THE REYES INCIDENT

BRIANA MORGAN

ISBN: 9798429131696

Briana Morgan
Atlanta, GA

www.BrianaMorganBooks.com

Trigger warnings: The following work contains scenes of graphic violence
including but not limited to dismemberment, disembowelment, stabbing,
drowning, and murder. Other sensitive subjects include vomiting, grief, death, post-
traumatic stress disorder, policing and arrests, divorce, infidelity, disability, child
death, sex, and explicit language. Reader discretion is advised.

To the families of Alex Dang, Claire Thibodeaux, and Ben and Ryan Jenkins. May you find peace.

DAWSONVILLE POLICE DEPARTMENT INCIDENT REPORT

CASE NO: 543
DATE: October 16, 2022
REPORTING OFFICER: N/A; Eyewitness Report
PREPARED BY: Officer Paul Wesson

DETAIL OF EVENT: Witness is female, Hispanic, approximately 24 years of age. Arrived at 22:36 EST on October 16, 2022. Witness appears disheveled. Possible injuries to chest, face, and mouth; possible internal bleeding. Witness declined medical assistance.

Witness claims to have knowledge surrounding the alleged disappearances of multiple Dawsonville residents aged 18 to approximately 25. Witness requested to speak with first available officer. Initial statement taken at 23:15 EST by Chief Roger Alameda. Further investigation required.

Witness escorted to Interview Room at 23:00

EST. Investigation pending by Sergeant Andrea McCollum.

ACTIONS TAKEN: Assigned to Sergeant McCollum by Chief Alameda. Sergeant McCollum to conduct an in-depth interview.

ANDIE

"Sergeant McCollum, you're being reassigned," Dad said.

I'd just gotten to the station, and the last thing I expected was for my father to corner me, let alone reassign me. I looked around at my colleagues, wondering why he'd selected me out of everyone else. The case I had been working on involved petty theft. It wasn't that I didn't think the theft crime was important, I just wasn't too psyched about it. So, the notion of reassignment piqued my interest.

My wife Joy and I had been having problems at home, too, and the theft case barely even distracted me from that. Whatever this new case was, maybe it had the potential to at least keep me from falling asleep at my desk.

"What about my current case?" I asked.

He hesitated. "Come to my office."

Not having much choice, I followed him. My steaming mug of coffee bounced as we walked, and I tried my best not to spill it. I wasn't clumsy, but my coordination certainly wasn't at its best this early in the morning.

Dad led me back to his office, which I could've found in the dark. You don't spend seven years at the same precinct without memorizing its interior layout. Someone had flung open the door, but I could still make out his name in golden letters on the outside: ROGER ALAMEDA, CHIEF, DAWSONVILLE POLICE DEPARTMENT. He'd been the chief for a long time, way back before I'd been born. It wouldn't have surprised me to learn he'd been the chief for centuries. Although he didn't look too old, he carried himself with wisdom. He was the kind of confident I wanted to become someday.

Dad gestured to the metal folding chair in front of his desk. "Please, sergeant, have a seat."

I set my mug down on the edge of his desk and sat. Dad shut his office door before coming around to the other side. He sat in his big wingback chair, rocking as he contemplated whatever he wanted to say.

"Have you... have you been keeping up with missing person reports?" he asked.

I frowned. Missing persons weren't typically my beat, and I'd only been involved in a handful of those cases through the years. As far as recent disappearances went, I didn't have a clue.

He must have known that.

"Not exactly," I offered.

"Hm." Dad stopped rocking and fixed me with a hard look. "What about reports of homicide?"

I leaned forward in my seat. "I've never covered homicide. I'm not exactly qualified—"

Dad waved me off. "You're qualified if I say you are. And I say you are, Andie. Gonna argue with me?"

"No, sir," I said. I didn't like where this was going. Icy fingers of dread dug into my stomach. He must have had a good reason if he wanted me to handle a homicide case. Wesson was much more qualified to handle this case, as he'd worked homicide for a decade. Even Hopewell would be better suited for this, and she only had two years of homicide experience.

With investigating murders, I was greener than the grass in front of the precinct.

"This case," said Dad, "is not one to be taken on lightly. I wouldn't reassign you if I didn't think you could handle it."

I nodded, though saying I felt less than confident would have been an understatement. My gaze drifted to the mug on his desk, still steaming, still untouched. Now, I felt too jittery to contemplate drinking coffee.

"Review the report and get back to me," he said. "If you have any doubts, conflicts of interest, or anything, I can give it to someone else, but I think you're the woman for the job. Do you trust me, Andie?"

I didn't have a choice, but yes, of course I did.

"I've looked over the case file, and this is gonna be a difficult one," Dad added. "Still, I wouldn't put you on it if I didn't think that it was something you could handle, all right?"

I sighed. He had a point. Although I was his daughter, I'd also been on the force long enough to handle almost anything. I'd proven myself, several times over. Surely whatever he had for me this time wouldn't be so different.

"She's waiting for you," he reiterated. "Might want to offer her coffee or something."

I nodded. The conversation as he saw it was over. I didn't bother asking any follow-up questions, and he didn't stop me as I got up and walked away. My dad had always been a man of few words. Working in the public sector improved his social skills some, but he still struggled with the ends of conversations.

For the most part, I hadn't inherited that trait. I hadn't been popular in high school, but I did well enough. I had friends. Now, as a police officer, I got along with most people. Even the criminals I brought in didn't hate me much. I tried to see all of them as people whose circumstances I could never fully understand. Whatever crime they committed was wrong, but that didn't mean they deserved to be treated as less of a person because of it.

Hell, we'd all done things that we weren't proud of. I didn't have the right to pass judgment on another person, just as they had no right to judge me.

Of course, not many people shared my worldview living in a small town.

Even before I spoke to Liv Reyes, I knew she'd gotten used to judgment. Although I had no idea what her story was about, her body language told me she was ready to be discredited—arms crossed, chin lowered, eyes staring straight ahead. Defiant.

I thought back to what Dad had told me in his office. This was a missing person case with notes of homicide. Was I well-equipped to handle anything like that, or was Dad setting me up to fail?

A muscle jerked in my jaw. I pushed the question away and got ready to do my damn job.

I found her in the first interview room sitting in a metal chair. Her dark eyes pierced a hole through me. I recognized that look —*distrust,* likely from previous encounters with the law.

I'd need to get through that to make her see me as a person. I just wanted to connect. I wanted to help. Once she understood that, I was sure we'd get along.

She stood when I walked in. I offered her my hand, and she shook it.

"Sergeant Andrea McCollum," I said.

"Olivia Reyes. Everyone calls me Liv." She sat, crossing her legs. Her clothes were clean—I recognized them as lost-and-found attire that had never been claimed—but the rest of her was not. A long, angry scratch ran across her right cheek, and blood flecked the edges of her mouth.

"Did they take your clothes?" I asked.

She nodded. "Said something about a lab."

Perfect. They were already looking for evidence.

"Do you need someone to take you to the hospital?" I asked.

"I'm not..." she trailed off, then tried again. "Most of this blood isn't mine. I want to tell you how it happened."

She winced, clutching her arm. Her face contorted in pain.

"You sure you don't need a medic?" I asked.

She shook her head. "I have fibromyalgia. It'll pass, I think."

I took the recorder out of my pocket and set it on the table between us. My finger hovered over the red button.

"Do you consent to being recorded?" I asked.

She smirked. "Would it matter if I didn't?"

I didn't answer. I hit RECORD. Liv shifted in her seat and cleared her throat.

"Sergeant Andrea McCollum recording eyewitness intake interview," I said. Then, to Liv: "Please restate your name for the record, Ms. Reyes."

"Olivia Reyes," she said again. "When can I start?"

"You can start now."

"This might be the strangest thing you've ever heard, but I have to put it out there. I have to get it out of me," she said. "I'm hoping this will give you cause to send someone out for a search. I don't know where to start."

I leaned forward in my chair. "Let's go with the beginning.

LIV

Yesterday's incident involved my friends—Alex Dang, Claire Thibodeaux, and Ben and Ryan Jenkins. Several years ago, Alex and Ryan got into urban exploration—trekking through abandoned shopping malls, condemned houses, the works. YouTube devoured their content. Alex and Ryan's channel was Urbexploitation. I shot videos for them before I moved away.

Everything started with Alex's text. He wanted me to meet him and Ryan in the woods. Growing up in Dawsonville, you hear shit about the forest. A bunch of kids in the nineties met out there to offer sacrifices to the devil. Satanic Panic stuff. There are also stories of people who went into the woods and never came out or people who came out screaming after seeing three-eyed deer. No one ever had proof.

Anyway, Alex texted me. He said if I was back in town, he and Ryan could use my camera skills. If Ryan had texted, I wouldn't have gone. Ryan, Alex, and I grew up in the same neighborhood, played together all the time when we were kids. Ryan and I dated in high school. We tried to stay together when I moved away for film school. It didn't work. I cheated on him. Naturally, he wasn't thrilled when he found out. We broke up, but he was still resentful. Whenever someone showed any interest in me, he talked shit to turn them against me. It sucked, but I couldn't do anything about it.

So, I grabbed my camera, laced up my shoes, and checked my battery levels. There weren't many places to charge in the middle of Dawsonville Forest.

Ryan's younger brother Ben was supposed to meet us there, too. Unlike Ryan, Ben didn't have his head up his ass. The only person I didn't know there was Claire. She replaced me as camerawoman when I went off to film school, so neither of us wanted to spend the day together.

As soon as I pulled up and got out of my car, Alex came over and hugged me. It was nice, like nothing had changed. Like Ryan hadn't tried a thousand times to come between us. I didn't see Ryan's car, and I understood why when he and Ben got out of Alex's van.

"Had to steal your mom's ride again?" I asked Alex.

He shook his head. "It's the only ride we have now. Rolled the Civic into a ditch."

"Jesus. Why didn't I hear about that?"

"Not my finest moment. I was checking my phone." He averted his gaze. "Channel notification. I keep the phone in the glove compartment now just to be safe."

Ryan looked at me but said nothing. Ben looked at Ryan and hesitated only briefly before hugging me as well.

"Long time no see," he said.

Alex was tall and well-built. Black stubble, sloping nose, sharp jawline, brown eyes. Korean. Handsome.

Ryan was shorter than Alex but wirier and leaner. Disheveled blonde hair, short on the sides and maybe a little too long on top. Blue eyes. The corners of his mouth turned down a little, making him look perpetually unhappy.

Ben looked nothing like his brother. He was taller than Ryan and Alex with an athletic build—he played basketball. He had floppy brown hair swept to one side and warm, brown eyes.

The boys replaced me with Claire after I went away. Looks-wise, she was gorgeous. She intimidated me. Claire was half French-Creole and half Irish. Her hair was curly and dark and fell over her shoulders. She had freckles across her cheeks and nose.

As far as I knew then, Claire didn't like me because Ryan had turned her against me. Like I said, he tried to do that with everyone since we broke up. Since Alex was his best friend, Ryan had bitched about me to Alex the most. Thankfully, Ryan treated me no differently than he had before the breakup.

When Alex introduced Claire, she didn't shake the hand I offered. Maybe if she had, we would've been friends sooner. Might've had more time together—or *better* time, at least.

After we'd all gathered, Ryan and Ben took the rafts and the air pump out of the trunk. Ben had a backpack strapped over his shoulders. It was army green and had his full name scribbled on the front flap in permanent marker.

We headed into the forest in silence. The woods were chilly. The cold aggravated my fibromyalgia, spreading pain through my joints and muscles. Finding the bunker took us a while, even with Alex's intel. It wasn't exactly top secret — I'd seen footage of it on the Internet.. Alex wanted to explore it all, to be the first to go all the way in.

The biggest danger was the region's radiation. Three-eyed deer, and all that. No one knew how dangerous the deeper parts of the bunker were, but Alex had a Geiger counter. He said he'd keep us posted. He said we wouldn't be in danger.

While we walked, he said he was grateful to have our help.

"Zipper Paranormal covered this place once," Alex said. "His results were inconclusive, but we're not looking for ghosts."

That's the thing about urban exploration: a lot of paranormal channels also explore abandoned places, but they're more interested in ghosts. Not Urbexploitation. It had never been like that.

The first part of the bunker was dry. It took a while to get to the flooded sections. The only sounds were dripping water, the hissing of Ryan's air raft dragging behind him, and our echoing footsteps. The second sound disappeared after Alex chastised

Ryan. He worried that dragging the raft might make holes, and then we couldn't use it.

The bunker's entrance sloped like a sunken driveway. Trucks, vans, and other military vehicles used to head down that way. It was prone to flooding, hence the rafts. Based on footage I'd seen, most of the bunker was underwater. We're talking five stories of a military base here, just submerged. I had thalassophobia, the fear of deep water.

I could swim, though. All of us could except Ben. When we were kids, he'd been the only one sitting out by the pool, focused on his tan or some book about sports. He must have been relieved about the rafts.

Claire and I readied our cameras. The boys set the rafts at the edge of the water. Ben held onto them so that they wouldn't float away. Alex ran a hand through his hair. His legs trembled like they always did when we filmed, and I was surprised he hadn't gotten past his childhood anxiety. When we were kids, he bit his nails, fidgeted, and bounced his leg a lot. Now, he wasn't biting his nails, but maybe he'd just outgrown that.

Claire and I exchanged a look.

Brow furrowed, I pointed my lens toward Alex.

"Hey," I said. "Who's filming this?"

"Both of you," he said. "We can go with the better angle."

Annoyance flared in my mind. He'd never doubted me before, and the challenge stung. I knew Claire had stepped into the spotlight, but I was determined not to let her show me up.

Claire opened her mouth like she had something to say, then changed her mind. She, too, raised her camera.

I sighed and started recording. Whatever Alex wanted, I'd make sure he got it.

Alex shoved his hands in his pockets. "Hey, explorers! It's Alex Dang. Once again, you're watching the antics of Urbexploitation. Don't try this at home."

Warmth rushes through my veins. The intro was familiar and

it comforted me. If I closed my eyes and shut out Claire, it was almost like nothing had changed.

"Today, we're in Dawsonville Forest," Alex continued. "We wanted to do something closer to home. This place is surrounded by rumors. From occult ceremonies during the Satanic Panic to mutated animals, radioactive waste, and more. There are plenty of reasons to stay away from it. As you can see, we're ignoring all those."

I readjusted my camera's focus, pulling back to get the rafts in view. Ben ended up in the shot, but he'd been in shots before. I doubted he minded or he wouldn't have come.

"Come with us," said Alex, "as we head into a flooded bunker and unravel the mysteries Dawsonville Forest has in store."

I cut. Claire kept filming, and it wasn't until Alex swept a hand across his neck that she realized what he wanted. That took me by surprise. She'd been filming them for years, but she didn't know them as well as I did.

We packed up the cameras and climbed aboard the rafts. Alex, Claire, and Ryan took one, and Ben and I got in the other. Jealousy flared in my chest. Maybe they didn't need me. Maybe they didn't like me as much as they liked Claire.

Ben picked up the oars paddled, taking us ahead of the others. I looked back at the other raft, hugging my camera close to my chest. Alex smiled at me. No one else paid me any attention.

"Reach into my backpack and grab the lights," Ben said.

The pack was sitting on the floor of the raft between his feet. I rummaged around inside it until my hand closed on cold metal. The lights looked like floodlights with big battery attachments. If they didn't fold up, they never would have fit into Ben's backpack.

"Good," Ben said. "Toggle the switch on the side of the packs and they should just come on. We can worry about placement once we know they're working."

I raised an eyebrow. "Since when do you know so much about lighting?"

"Since our best lighting tech went off to film school," he said.

I guessed that meant Claire had less experience than I did, too. Without saying anything, I switched the lights on. They were harsh and yellow, reflecting off the surface of the water like the sun. Ben cursed. I directed the light away from him, pointing forward into the bunker.

After a few adjustments, we were ready to film. I raised the camera and started recording. Alex sat as straight as he could and beamed into the lens.

"As you can see, this bunker's treacherous. We have to contend with about five stories or more of water, plus uncertain lighting conditions." Alex pushed his hair off his forehead. He stared at Claire. When she didn't do anything, he sighed. "Can you get some shots up ahead? Liv has me covered. I want to make sure we're setting the scene."

Claire grumbled something but did what he asked anyway. I wondered how often she'd been told to focus on their surroundings. I'd been working with the boys so long that I had no trouble anticipating what they wanted shots to look like. But Claire had been with them for the past three years. I assumed she had learned something.

Ryan scooted forward to peer over Alex's shoulder. Back when I'd been the primary camerawoman, they did the intros for each video together. I wondered why they'd changed it, why they'd felt the need to fix things that hadn't been broken. Honestly, I was still nursing the hurt I felt at having been replaced. I had taken the job of my own free will, but it still bothered me that the future was so up in the air. When Alex contacted me, he hadn't made it seem like a partnership was coming. No long-term deal or anything. We hadn't even drawn up a contract.

Ryan leaned around Alex and cleared his throat. "Our cellphones don't work here, either. If anything happens to us, we can't call for help. We've filmed in dangerous locations before, but at least we could call someone in an emergency."

I thought back to a video we'd made in an abandoned mental

hospital. We had to haul our asses up to Kentucky. Ryan and I had both contracted a stomach bug; we couldn't stop puking. Three days into the trip, we were shaky, dehydrated, and could barely stay awake. Alex called us an ambulance even though we were in the middle of nowhere. Luckily, all we'd needed were saline drip IVs, and it was a huge relief to know we weren't as alone there as we'd felt upon arriving.

I checked my phone. No service. We were on our own.

Ryan and Alex touched on the history of the bunker. It had been owned and operated by the military up until the 1950s, when it was suddenly abandoned. No one had found any records explaining why the bunker wasn't used anymore. It had flooded from decades of rainfall, disrepair, and disuse.

As Ben paddled, I kept filming. So did Claire. Ryan and Alex talked until there was nothing left to say. We headed deeper and deeper into the bunker, until we couldn't see the entrance anymore. The floodlights kept us going. We were all okay.

Maybe they'd all be here with me if it weren't for the light in the water.

The light wasn't ours. It wasn't a reflection. For one thing, it was cooler, a far cry from the yellow glare of our floodlights. It was submerged, and it kept moving. If we'd been somewhere else, I might have thought it was a fish. But the bunker was too isolated and too hostile for anything to survive there.

I had to know what was down there. Without stopping to think, I plunged my hand into the water. The chill made my bones ache. Right before I closed my hand around the light, it darted away.

"What are you doing?" Ben asked.

"I thought I saw something," I said. "Looked like a light or something."

"It wasn't a reflection?"

"No, Ben," I snapped. "I don't think so."

I felt bad for being short with him, but I was sick of the boys dismissing me. In the past, whenever I thought I'd seen something, they teased me.

I leaned over the edge of the raft and peered into the water.

The light came back brighter than before. Closer, too.

The urge to reach into the water again overpowered me despite the cold.

"Film her," Alex said to Claire. He gestured to Ryan, and Ryan picked up his paddle.

"Wait a sec." Ben raised a hand, holding Ryan off. "We don't want to scare it off."

"We don't even know what it is," I said.

"Exactly," said Ben. "And if we're talking and splashing around so much, we'll never get the chance to."

I wish he'd been right. I wish we could've scared them off.

Just as I reached toward the water again, the first one broke the surface.

I didn't understand what I was seeing. It looked a whole lot like a human, but pure white. Not just pale, but white, like Cloroxed bones. Her face was feminine, with two eyes, a nose, and a mouth. She had a light in her forehead. It reminded me of those fish that live at the bottom of the ocean, anglerfish.

Her long black hair billowed around her shoulders in the water. I couldn't see for sure, but it seemed like she was naked. I thought she had black lipstick on, too, and when she smiled, her teeth were pointed.

I reeled backward into Ben's lap. The paddle slipped out of his hands, plunged into the water, and vanished.

Ben swore.

When the woman laughed. Her voice sounded like water running over stones.

"Looks like you kids are lost," she said.

I couldn't do anything but gape at her.

"Who are you?" Alex blurted out.

The woman's gaze flicked to Alex. Her eyes were silver. Like the back of a mirror. It looked like they'd been lined with heavy black makeup, but it was just her skin.

Before she could answer, two more figures popped out of the water on either side of her. It scared me so bad I almost toppled out of the raft entirely. They looked like the first woman, though one had blue hair and the other bright red. Not ginger, but red. The color of blood. She also struck me as the leader.

"She's Molly," said the woman with the red hair. "My sister."

"And who the hell are you?" Alex pressed. I couldn't believe how he was speaking to them. It was like he wasn't scared out of his mind, and maybe he wasn't. Not yet. But I'd known Alex Dang long enough to know that this kind of thing should've spooked him.

"I'm Harper," she answered. "That's Sidney. What are you doing down here?"

Harper was sleek and pale, almost the color of marble. Her eyes were blue with slitted pupils, and her lips were black. Her teeth were sharp, but not as formidable as Molly's. Her ears were long, too, almost like fins. Her fingers were webbed. Her hair was long and crimson.

Like Harper, Sidney was sleek and pale, almost the color of marble. Her eyes were green with slitted pupils, and her lips were also black. Her teeth were sharp and thin like needles. She had silver stripes going down her face and her sides. Her tail was blue threaded with silver, like a barracuda's. It matched her long hair.

"Fuck," Ryan said. "Maybe we shouldn't be here."

"We should leave," said Ben.

I was thinking the same thing. I don't know why we didn't.

"I'm still recording all of this," Claire said to Alex. "You never told me to stop."

I told myself that Molly must have gotten lost in the bunker somehow. It was easier to believe that when there had been only one of her. Three was a hard sell.

Before the other ones showed up, I had thought we needed to

get Molly some help. I didn't think Molly was her real name, but it was all she'd given us to go on, so it would have to do.

"Are you... do you live down here?" I asked.

"Stuck in the water," Harper said. "Can't get up and go anywhere."

I glanced at Alex. He frowned, eyebrows knitting together as he looked the trio over. Like me, I assumed he was trying to make sense of what we were seeing.

"You're stuck?" Ryan echoed.

"I think we should keep our distance," Ben said.

Harper smiled and flipped over in the water. She floated on her back, staring up at the ceiling a hundred feet above us. Her breasts came into view, along with her toned abdominal muscles and the full length of her tail. It was striped red, white, and brown, with spines jutting out like a lionfish. It looked like she had spines coming off it. The spines were barbed. I didn't want to learn how sharp they were.

"Keep filming," Alex hissed.

Harper smiled. Her teeth looked sharp, but maybe that was the lighting or the potential radiation. How long had she been down there? Long enough to mutate?

Goddamn mermaids. That's what we were dealing with. I almost couldn't believe it, but what else could Harper, Molly, and Sidney be? The evidence was there. I didn't fully understand the power dynamics at play, but I knew enough to realize that Harper was in control.

"You're filming us?" Molly asked.

"How... you know what filming is?" Alex asked.

"They used to record us all the time," Molly said. "Their instruments looked different. Clunkier. But they do the same thing, yes?"

"Yes," Ryan answered.

I didn't know who *they* were, but I pushed it to the back of my mind. The sirens had given us their blessing, so, we'd roll with it.

Claire kept her camera trained on them. I still held mine, but I wasn't using it. Somehow, it didn't seem right. Ryan and Alex exchanged a look.

Alex waved a hand at Claire. "She'll only film with your permission. If you're not cool with anything, just let us know."

He looked pointedly at me. I hesitated.

It wasn't like I hadn't filmed weird shit before. A lot of the locations we'd visited we hadn't obtained a permit to travel to, let alone record. We'd received some cease and desist letters from various property owners. Most of it had been tame, but there were still a few weirdos we'd gotten in the frame, people we hadn't gotten to sign release forms. Those that recognized themselves were seldom understanding. And all those people had been human.

I didn't think crossing the mermaids or sirens or whatever was a good idea.

"I'm only filming if you want me to," I said to Harper. There were more important things to worry about at that moment than whatever Alex and Ryan wanted. I was trying not to get us hurt, or killed. We still didn't understand what we were up against.

"We don't mind," Harper said. She looked at the others, who only nodded. Sidney's gaze was warm as it touched me. Molly grinned, her mouth full of needles. I sucked in a breath.

If we couldn't stay on their good side, who knew what might happen?

"I like the attention," Sidney added.

Still, Molly said nothing.

Harper swam parallel to our raft, rolling onto her back in the water. The light glanced off the rivulets that slid over her skin.

"We don't mind you filming," Harper said again, "as long as you play by our rules."

She raked her eyes over me, lingering on my neck. I fought the urge to cover it.

Alex leveled his gaze at her. "We're in your neck of the woods. I guess whatever you say goes."

Harper grinned again. Fear squeezed my stomach.

"We should head to deeper water. That's easier for us. And I'll bet the lighting is better."

This was a bad idea. Every fiber of my being screamed it. I was in pain, for one thing. The fatigue would hit me soon. Chronically tired people aren't thrilled about swimming.

"Deeper water," Alex echoed.

"How would the lighting be better?" Ryan asked.

Harper's smile dimmed. "There's a hole in the ceiling, and sunlight comes in. Why, don't you trust me?"

"I... it's not that," Alex stammered. "Ryan's just... we just had different plans for the shoot."

"Plans change," Sidney said, almost dreamily.

Molly kept staring at us, saying nothing. Something flickered in her eyes.

I wanted to say something to Alex. I wanted to tell him I had a bad feeling, that maybe we shouldn't trust these creatures. But he just looked at me and nodded, and I knew I didn't have a choice.

"Okay," said Ryan. "You all lead the way."

More than anything, I wish I'd said something to stop them.

I don't know how it happened, but we let them push the rafts. I thought it was a terrible idea, letting them lead us, but Alex insisted. Ryan went along with it like he went along with everything. I should've said something when no one else did. I guess it doesn't matter now.

For a minute, I looked back at Ben. His brow was creased like he was lost in thought, maybe thinking of a way to protest without coming across as a party pooper. He might've been on my side had I done anything.

Harper was at the back of our raft. Sidney and Molly were at the other. Harper kept talking, either to fill the silence or simply because she liked the sound of her voice. Or both.

"Been abandoned down here for a long time," she said. "No one down here until you all came along. Well, no one besides the three of us."

I remember thinking how weird it was that she said that. From the footage posted on YouTube and TikTok of other people around our age exploring the bunker, I doubted she was telling the truth. Maybe we'd just gotten farther than anyone else, but maybe not.

Still, I knew Alex had seen the footage, too. When I looked back at him, something flashed in his eyes—right before Ryan interrupted.

"How did you end up down here, anyway?" he asked.

"We used to be like you," Harper said. "I guess you must have a device that measures radiation? It should tell you how dangerous it is to stay down here too long. That's what happened to us. We should have gotten out sooner."

I knew that wasn't right. I knew it couldn't be right, even back then.

"How long?" I asked.

Harper considered me for a minute. Maybe she was sizing me up. "Long enough, little fish. We used to have legs. Used to have to come up for air when we were swimming here, too."

"Good thing you could all swim," said Ben. "If I got stuck here, I'd be screwed."

I looked at Claire. She was still rolling, still recording it all. It felt petty, but I couldn't help wondering if my footage would be better than hers. It wasn't like I had to prove myself to the boys anymore, but I couldn't help being competitive. I wanted to be back on top.

The sirens turned us down a shadowy corridor. Even though we had lighting with us, it barely seemed to break through the darkness of the bunker. Our raft bumped into something floating on the water. I leaned over the edge to get a closer look.

An empty water bottle, faded stickers on the side and the name CLARA scrawled on it in permanent marker, floated in the water. This was proof people besides us had been in the bunker, which we could confront the sirens with.

It didn't seem like the others thought they were lying. I

wanted to bring it up but I couldn't figure out how without alerting the sirens. I didn't want them thinking I was onto them. I didn't know exactly what I was afraid of—whether they'd retaliate or something. I just knew that I was afraid and that we needed to be careful.

They brought us deeper into the bunker. Deeper than we ever should've gone. Deeper than anyone needed to go.

From: **Andrea McCollum** <amccollum@dpd.gov>
To: **Roger Alameda** <ralameda@dpd.gov>
Subject: **The Reyes Incident**

Mon, October 17, 2022, 1:43 PM

Chief,

I've attached a preliminary report for your consideration. This case should be escalated to the Georgia Bureau of Investigation. I'll keep gathering information so that we can plan the next steps. In the meantime, I'd like to take Officer Lyle off her current case to consult on this one. I trust her judgment.

Let me know what you think. As always, I value your opinion.

Best,

Sergeant McCollum

From: **Roger Alameda** <ralameda@dpd.gov>
To: **Andrea McCollum** <amccollum@dpd.gov>
Subject: **RE: The Reyes Incident**

Wed, October 19, 2022, 1:27 PM

Sergeant McCollum,

Sorry for the delay. Regarding your request to pull Lyle off her case, I'm granting you permission under one condition: you present concrete, tangible evidence to corroborate Reyes's report. I'd also like her to undergo psychiatric evaluation and a drug test to rule out psychosis or an adverse reaction to illegal substances. If you are unable to provide this proof, I'll write off her testimony as hearsay unless we hear from an outside party.

For now, there's also no need to bring in the GBI. You know how I feel about them.

If you need more resources or opinions on this, you know where to find me.

Regards,

Chief Alameda

From: **Roger Alameda** <ralameda@dpd.gov>
To: **Andrea McCollum** <amccollum@dpd.gov>,
Clarissa Lyle <clyle@dpd.gov>
Subject: ***URGENT* Case Reassignment Detail**

Fri, October 21, 2022, 1:45 PM

Sergeant McCollum and Officer Lyle,

Effective tomorrow, you will be collaborating
on the Reyes case. Officer Lyle, Sergeant
McCollum will fill you in on the details.
I've also attached a preliminary incident
report to this email.

Sergeant McCollum, remember what I said about
tangible proof.

Officer Lyle, let me know whom you'd like to
take over on that armed robbery situation.
You've made a lot of headway there and I hate
to pull you off this case, but I agree with
Sergeant McCollum. Your judgment is solid.

Yours,

Alameda

ANDIE

"Hi, Ms. Reyes," my partner said. "My name is Officer Lyle. I'll be assisting Sergeant McCollum with this case. Can I call you Olivia?"

"Liv, please," she insisted.

"Liv, then. It's nice to meet you."

"Likewise."

Liv reached up and rubbed the back of her neck. Was she hurting again?

Lyle and I sat across the table from Liv. I'd filled my partner in on everything pertaining to the case so far, and I looked forward to seeing what insights she'd provide regarding Liv's interview.

"I looked over the police report Officer Wesson filed last week, as well as all the transcripts of your original statement," Lyle said. "Today, we'd like to hear part of your statement again to see if anything's changed."

Lyle checked her notes. "I'd like to ask you about the sirens you described. Early on, you said you had reservations about them."

"Reservations. That's putting it mildly." Liv glanced at Lyle, who was still reading, before she continued. "They terrified me, and I felt an immense sense of dread when I looked at them."

I sipped my coffee. "Where did they take you?"

She gestured to my cup. "Can you bring me some of that first?"

LIV

Harper was right about the light. Inside the lair, there was a huge hole in the ceiling, and sunlight shone down on the slab and the water.

We got out of the rafts and climbed onto the slab. Ryan pointed out different shots for Claire to get. He'd always been a micromanager. Alex was talking to Ben. Even standing on concrete, Ben was nervous about being surrounded by so much water. Alex kept fidgeting, alternating shoving his hands in his pockets and taking them out again. He rocked back and forth on his eyes, his eyes never leaving the water's surface.

As I looked around the concrete slab, I noticed something off. There was a bundle in the back, just out of the light, covered with a tarp. It didn't look like it belonged. I'm not sure how else to explain it except to say that it felt *wrong*. I went over to the tarp; I had to know what it was hiding. I lifted the edge of it and peeled it back.

Underneath the tarp was a big pile of bones. They were a nasty grayish color. I can't get that color out of my head. I took my phone out of my pocket, hands shaking, and took a picture. The phone's flash lit up everything.

My stomach rolled. There were marks on the bones. Grooves.

Almost like someone had bitten them—or some*thing* with knife-edged teeth.

I was about to turn around to show my friends the bones, but before I could, the sirens started singing.

Their song didn't have any words. It was just tones. The three of them harmonized, and it made the hairs at the nape of my neck stand up and chills run down my arms. I looked over at Alex. He was staring straight ahead, his eyes wide and glassy. I'd never seen him look like that before. I looked over at Ryan and Ben to find them wearing similar expressions.

Claire's face was pale. She met my gaze, and her eyes shone with unshed tears. Alex, Ryan, and Ben kept looking at the sirens in the water, their jaws slack. It was unnerving. Then, the sirens drifted off.

The boys dropped to the concrete slab as if they'd been shot. I ran over to Alex. His eyes were closed. I pressed my hand against his neck to check his pulse, and he was just sleeping. Still, it was weird.

Claire checked Ben while I checked Ryan. They were all the same. I shook all of them to try to get them to wake up — Ryan used to be such a light sleeper — but none of them stirred. Claire and I looked at each other. The sirens stopped singing.

That was when they popped the rafts.

Claire stared straight ahead like she hadn't even heard them. My heart was in my throat. We couldn't get out of there without swimming, and I knew the minute we went in the water, we were done for.

"What do they want?" Claire asked.

It was then that I realized I was the only one who knew about the bones. I hadn't seen any fish or anything besides them down there, which meant pickings had to be slim for them. But they were eating something, and I knew that I was the only one in our group who understood the truth: the sirens were going to eat us. We must have looked like a Thanksgiving feast to them. The minute they saw us, they probably started scheming to kill us.

I knew we were going to die. They were going to kill us, whatever they were.

We would have tried to come up with an escape plan, but there was nothing we could talk about or do without Harper, Molly, and Sidney hearing. Slowly, the trio circled the platform. Part of me hoped they'd get tired of waiting. A bigger part knew they wouldn't.

"You don't know how I grew up," Claire said, "but I lived in a haunted house. I *know* it was haunted. At the time, I tried to talk myself out of everything I saw, tried to come up with some logical explanation for everything that happened, when maybe... there was never a logical explanation. Maybe that's what's happening here."

I kept looking at the boys. In the wake of an adrenaline crash, I felt exhausted. When I looked back at Claire, her eyelids drooped. She yawned.

"We need to stay awake," I said, because I didn't know what the sirens might do to us if we didn't.

"How?" she asked.

"I don't know. I guess we just keep talking."

Claire nodded, but she didn't say anything else right away.

"Tell me how you started working for the boys," I prompted. After all, I only knew the basics, and I couldn't think of anything better for us to talk about.

Claire looked out at the water. "They put an ad on Craigslist. Kinda thought I was going to get murdered."

I frowned. That didn't seem like Ryan and Alex's style.

"I thought they put up a video ad on their channel or something," I said.

"Nah. They wanted someone local. I guess Craigslist was easier."

"I didn't know anyone used Craigslist anymore."

"I think it's just me."

We smiled at each other. It wasn't anything major, but it made me feel more human. It made me feel like everything wasn't going to shit for a minute.

I rested my hands on my thighs. "I went away to film school. Did they tell you that?"

"Yes," Claire said. "They told you... they told me a lot about you."

I'd expected as much, but hearing it confirmed wasn't as satisfying as I'd thought. I wished I'd been around to defend myself to Claire against whatever the boys—especially Ryan—had said while I was gone.

"I was jealous," Claire said. "Maybe I still am. Of you, I mean."

My eyebrows shot up. "Jealous?"

Claire touched her hair. "I was... I resented you, especially in the beginning."

I blinked. It wasn't what I'd expected her to say.

"Resented me?" I asked.

"Your relationship with them. How long you'd known them and everything." She sighed. "You were just...everywhere. They couldn't stop talking about you. Even when they said some questionable things, you could tell they still cared about you. There was history. That's something I don't have with them."

"But you will," I said and meant it.

"If we get out of here," she added.

I pressed my lips together. I didn't want to die. I didn't want them to eat me. But we didn't have much choice.

"I dropped out of film school," I said. It felt good to put it out there. I hadn't told anyone else. I was too afraid of admitting that I'd failed. "I just... I couldn't do it anymore. I hated how rigid the program was, and how self-absorbed everyone was."

"Alex said you wanted to be a filmmaker," Claire said.

"Yeah," I said.

"But you dropped out of school?"

"I didn't belong there. But... I don't belong here, either, and I don't know what to do."

"You could still make a movie," Claire said.

"If we get out of here," I echoed.

The silence of the bunker settled on my skin. Water lapped at the edges of the slab. I looked over at the books, but they were still asleep. Claire followed my gaze, frowning.

"I've seen your work," I admitted. "Their videos you filmed. You do a good job."

"Thank you." She paused. "I was mad at Alex for inviting you, you know. I'm not proud of it, but I was. I feel like all of this is somehow my fault, like I put all this negative energy out there."

"You know that's not true," I said.

"I thought maybe they wanted you back here for good."

I shook my head. "No way. Ryan can't stand me."

"For what it's worth," Claire said, "Ryan's immature."

We seemed to reach a truce then. Maybe when—or even *if*—we made it out of here alive, we could spend more time together. Maybe we'd be friends.

After we talked, we felt hopeful, and I think the sirens could sense it. I think that was why they attacked us.

Harper lunged out of the water like a dolphin. She grabbed Ben's arm and pull him off the slab. Claire and I rushed to help him, but Harper was too fast. Sidney and Molly joined her, the three of them holding Ben. He snapped awake and screamed.

He couldn't swim. He didn't stand a chance. I was about to dive into the water and try to pull him out of their grasp, but Claire stopped me.

"You can't," she said. "It's too dangerous."

I fought the urge to argue. She was right—the sirens would've hurt me, too. They wanted to hurt all of us. Just because they started with Ben didn't mean they'd stop.

The sirens tore Ben to pieces. Harper grabbed one arm. Molly grabbed the other. Sidney held his body steady. Claire and I watched, horrified, as they pulled him apart. The arm came off with a wet, ripping sound that made my stomach churn. I saw it. All of it. I watched it unfold. Even now, talking about it, I can see the incident replaying in my head. It just might be the most traumatic thing that I have ever seen. The jury's still out on that one, though.

Blood bloomed in the water. There was another sick, wet, tearing sound. I had to look away.

Claire wept. I wished I could have.

Andie

I pulled a double shift and got home late Sunday night. Joy was fast asleep, snoring on the couch when I came in. The lamp on the end table was on, and the television murmured, its light flickering over Joy's features.

Yawning, I crossed the room to touch her shoulder. I shook her and she stirred.

"What?" Joy asked.

"I'm home," I said. "Sorry it's so late. Did you wait up for me?"

"I tried to." She sat up on the couch, rubbing her eyes. "How was work?"

"Not the best." Since we'd been married for a decade, Joy knew better than to ask me about the particulars of a case, even when she wanted to know. She knew that I couldn't divulge them. Most of the time, I followed that directive. Still, with a case as weird as Liv's bunker, the best plan was to keep quiet. What Joy didn't know wouldn't hurt her.

"How are the kids?" I asked. I hadn't asked about them in a while, and I felt guilty about it. I hadn't even thought about Joy at work last week.

Joy taught art at Dawsonville Elementary School. Now, it didn't seem to make any difference what she did. If she was happy

—and she was, as far as I could tell—I didn't care what she did. Working for the force, I made enough money for us to live comfortably on. A promotion and a raise wouldn't hurt, but those were both a long time coming.

Neither of us brought those things up, either. We were better off for it. There were a lot of things we just didn't talk about anymore.

Joy tucked a strand of strawberry blonde hair behind her ear. When we first started dating, I thought that this was the cutest thing that I had ever seen. This far into our relationship, I hardly noticed when she did it.

"One of them tried to eat paint today," she said. "Doubt that happens at your job."

"You'd be surprised." I smirked, sitting beside her on the couch. This close, I could see the bags under her eyes, the dark circles there.

"What are you looking at me like that for?" she asked.

"You haven't been sleeping," I said. "Why don't you take the bed tonight and let me have the couch?"

Joy sighed. "That's not what we agreed on, and it's not fair to you."

"Who cares what we agreed on?" I asked, even though I did. "I can run on next to nothing. There's plenty of mediocre coffee at the station. You, on the other hand, are teaching our nation's future."

Joy pressed her lips together. "You're sure you don't mind?"

"I don't mind," I answered, even though I did. "It's a school night. I insist."

She'd been sleeping on the couch for the past two months, and I couldn't believe I was only now noticing how much it had affected her. Then again, perhaps I had, and I just hadn't cared.

Serves her right, a small, evil part of me mused. It was a part I wasn't proud of that I hadn't been able to shake, not since Joy's admission about what had happened at the school's open house.

"Open house doesn't mean open legs," I'd shouted. "You can't just go out and get drunk with a coworker. You can't sleep with him and turn off your phone all night. Joy, I was worried. Joy, I didn't think..." At a loss for words, I'd had to let my voice trail off. I never thought she'd cheat.

"Fine," she said, even though I knew it wasn't. "How's Roger, by the way?"

Dad had been a pillar of the Dawsonville community. He'd caught Joy and me having sex in the back of my Corolla in high school and had let us off with just a warning. In a town as small as ours was, he made sure no one found out. No matter what happened between us at work, I'd never forget that kindness. He'd offered me my job at graduation.

"You'll make enough to put bread on the table for your young one," he'd said. I couldn't refuse. After all, it wasn't like Joy could make some money, not when she had no diploma and our newborn son to care for. The son that wasn't mine, that I had never even wanted.

The son who had reminded me I shared Joy with a *man*.

I glanced at the side table. There was a picture of us holding Tyler there, a broken line across the glass. The black plastic frame was chipped on the corner. A pang of regret stabbed my chest, and I wish I'd never thrown it. If anything had happened to the photograph itself, I would never have forgiven myself. Joy wouldn't have forgiven me, either.

In the picture, we look happy. I think that was the last time we were.

"It's coming up," Joy said, as if I could forget the worst day of my life.

"Five years," I said, my throat thick with phlegm, choked with emotion. "Do you... I mean, did you want to do something?"

"Why?" she asked. "To celebrate it? To commemorate it? No, thank you."

Joy got up from the couch and went into the kitchen. She opened and shut a few cabinets.

"You won't find it," I told her. "I threw it out."

"Threw what out?" she asked, moving on to rummage through everything in the pantry.

"The whiskey, Joy," I said. "Did you think I wouldn't find it?"

My wife freezes and the kitchen goes quiet. It feels like the whole house is still.

"You promised me it wouldn't happen anymore," I said.

"I was saving it," she said.

"For a special occasion?" I asked. "Do you expect me to believe that? At this point, it's insulting."

I got up from the couch and stood in the kitchen doorway. Joy leaned against the front of the refrigerator with her forehead against the stainless steel. Her arms were folded in front of her chest, and she didn't look up when I entered. I knew she could see me. She was just being stubborn. She was always stubborn when she knew that I was right.

"You can't keep shutting me out," I said. "We agreed we'd try to make this work. We agreed *twice*."

"I don't know what you want from me," she said.

I exhaled through my nose. "I want to talk through this, Joy. I don't want to feel like I'm just hitting my head against the wall trying to get through to you. Don't you want that?"

She put her face in her hands. "I don't know what I want anymore."

"Then you'd better figure it out."

I turned and walked away, leaving her in the kitchen. I had more important things to worry about than her. If she wasn't willing to make our marriage work, maybe it was already past the point of repairing. Maybe, like a dog, I should just take it out back and shoot it.

W hen I got to the station the next morning, the rain was coming down in sheets. Despite whatever agreement I assumed we'd reached, Joy had slept on the couch again. Now, I was thankful to have gotten a good night's sleep. I'd need it for the day to come.

Dad greeted me at the door, which didn't bode well for the morning. He held a steaming mug of coffee in one hand and a hefty file in the other.

"Morning," I greeted him.

"Andie," he said. "There's been a new development. Have you heard anything?"

A new development since the previous day? On a case this strange? The sinking feeling in my gut told me it wasn't good. Wordlessly, I shook my head.

"I was afraid of that," he said. "Come with me. I'll tell you everything."

I swallowed the lump in my throat. I followed the chief back to the interrogation rooms, half expecting to see Liv Reyes there. Instead, I saw two women that I didn't recognize. They sat on one side of the table staring down at photographs spread across the surface.

I looked at Dad. "Are they part of my case?"

"They are now, Andie. Look," he started, "I wish I'd called you earlier to brief you. I would have if I could. But I've been here all night. I've been talking to these two since they got here around one a.m. You're looking at someone's parents, Andie."

"Liv's parents?"

"No." Dad reached up and scratched the back of his neck. He only did that when he was nervous, and I'd seldom seen him nervous. "Ariel and Iris Thibodeaux. That last name ring any bells?"

"Shit," I said in a low voice. "Claire's moms, I'm guessing."

"We're... we're still trying to recover her body, Andie," he said.

"Jesus." I clenched and unclenched my fists at my side. I half expected him to play the lesbian card again here. "You can't put someone else on this one?"

"You have the most relevant experience, plus you're on Liv's case already," he said. "I debated going with Lyle, but she..."

A pained look crossed Dad's face. I watched him, waiting for it to pass, but it never did. He sighed.

"Remind me," I said. Guilt twisted my gut. I should've known this part of my partner's life, but I didn't. It had happened before I met her.

"Her kid went missing years ago," he said. "Similar… circumstances. It's complicated."

"How long ago?"

"Ten years."

"Ever find a body?"

"No." He rubbed the back of his neck again. "Now, do you see why I was reluctant to even put her on the Reyes case? I can't ask her to do this, too. I can't make her relive the worst time of her life, Andie. I won't."

This case had just gotten a whole lot more complicated than I felt equipped to handle. I debated asking to have Lyle go into the interview room with me, but I hadn't seen her yet, and for all I knew she wasn't even coming into work today. Shit.

"No dead kid cases, Dad." My throat tightened, and I felt like crying just saying the words. "You promised me I wouldn't have to."

"I know," he said. "I'm sorry."

I appreciated him for not mentioning Tyler. Most days, I didn't even think about him, but maybe the conversation I'd had with Joy the night before, coupled with the approaching anniversary, had affected me more than I thought.

"I believe what Liv has told us so far," I told him. "Keeping that in mind, it's… it's not likely we'll find anything—*anyone*—alive. Maybe not even bodies. You know that, right?"

"I wouldn't ask you to do this if I didn't need you to," Dad said. "Get in there and do your job. Compartmentalize. I'm sorry, but we don't have the resources to assign someone else to this case. Even if we did, you're the best person to handle it."

His praise didn't make me feel any better.

"You don't have to like it. Just do your job."

Before I could say anything I'd regret, I took the file from him and walked into the room. Both women looked up when I entered. One was white and very blonde, with blue eyes that pierced me like a needle pinning a moth to a corkboard. Her wife was Black, with long hair braided over her shoulders. Her dark brown eyes shone with tears, though they were kinder than her wife's.

"Mrs. and Mrs. Thibodeaux," I started. "I'm so sorry for your —" Abruptly, I cut myself off. *I'm so sorry for your loss,* I'd almost said. Like an idiot. We hadn't found a body. We didn't know for sure that Claire was dead, despite what my gut and Liv Reyes had told me.

"I'm Ariel," said the white woman, saving me from putting my foot down my throat. "And this is Iris. Our daughter is..." Her voice trailed off, and she finally looked away from me.

Iris squeezed her hand. "Our daughter is missing."

I set the file folder on the table and opened it in front of them. I could see a few of the photographs they'd brought, and they made grief twist my heart. I swallowed hard and, despite already knowing the answer, I asked, "How long ago?"

Iris looked down at the row of photographs. "Nine days."

"Can I ask why you waited so long to report her missing?" I asked.

Ariel glared at me. "You can't be blaming us right now."

"Not blaming," I said, because I wasn't. "I just need to learn more about Claire's habits, whether she's done this kind of thing before, if you're not always in touch, et cetera."

"We have ideas," Iris said. "Maybe some leads you can follow."

"I'm all ears," I said.

Ariel and Iris studied each other, and a look passed between them. I knew it well from my own marriage. Both were trying not to let on how terrified they were, along with how little they trusted me. I didn't blame them.

As a queer woman, I knew how hard it was for anyone in Dawsonville to live authentically. These women were not only doing that but also seeking help from an institution that often discriminated against them. I wanted to believe Dad wasn't part of that—Dad, or anyone else that I knew—but I wasn't that naïve. Even a little could slip in and turn into something evil.

I'm a lesbian, I wanted to tell them. *I understand what you're going through*. But maybe the second part wasn't quite true. I had lost a child, but not the same way. I hadn't held out hope that he'd come back.

I pressed my lips together and waited for them to keep talking.

"She has a job as a... she records videos," Ariel explained. "For some local kids. They wander into abandoned buildings, condemned barns, places like that."

"We don't know them well," Iris said. "The people she works for. Or with."

I had to act like I didn't know exactly who she meant. Liv's statement hadn't been corroborated yet. Besides that, I didn't want to give Claire's mothers false hope. I'd have to wait for tangible proof of what had happened to their daughter.

Liv

Ryan and Alex came to while the sirens were tearing Ben apart. His screams echoed off the walls of the bunker, too loud to ignore. Alex's eyes snapped open, and he looked to me first. I was too in shock to say anything to him.

"Ben," Alex said.

Ryan tried to get to his feet and stumbled. When he noticed the commotion in the water—when he fully realized what was happening to his brother—an anguished cry tore from his throat.

"Ryan," Claire said.

Alex stood, his legs trembling.

Ryan tried to fling himself into the water.

Claire, Alex, and I grabbed whatever parts of him we could reach and struggled to keep him firmly planted on dry land. I pulled a muscle in my shoulder. Ryan was screaming, sobbing, and tearing at his clothes and hair. If I hadn't been in shock, I might've reacted the same way. Mostly, I was trying not to look down at the blood that spread across the water. I couldn't see the sirens anymore. They must have taken their prize somewhere they could eat it—*him*—easier.

I couldn't get Ben's terror-stricken face out of my head, nor the terrible sounds of his limbs coming off. I let go of Ryan to puke over the edge of the platform. Claire followed suit. I don't know how Alex's stomach stayed strong, but he kept his grip on Ryan and murmured encouragement to him I couldn't quite make out.

Claire helped me sit on the platform. My legs shook so badly I never could've managed it alone. I appreciated having Claire there with me. As I looked past her to Alex and Ryan, I noticed Ryan was pale and his knees were locked.

"He's gonna faint," I told Alex.

Alex tugged Ryan backward. Ryan staggered and fell to his knees. Alex went down with him, catching himself before he could fall flat on his face. It was close.

"I'm here," Alex kept saying to Ryan. "I'm not going anywhere. I promise."

Ryan's cries were hiccupping sobs that racked his whole body. Silent tears made Alex's cheeks shine as well. I was certain I was crying, too. Seeing my friends in so much pain was enough to finally break me.

"Hey," Alex tried again. Ryan put his face in his hands and screamed again. The sharpness of it cut me as it echoed off the walls. I'd never heard anyone scream like that before.

"I can't, I can't, I can't," Ryan mumbled. "Can't lose, can't lose—"

"Shh," said Alex, rubbing his back. "Shh, man. Listen, we can get through this."

I didn't think we could. I didn't think Alex even believed what he was saying. I'm sure Claire didn't either. Ryan stilled, though. He lowered his hands from his face.

"I love you," he said softly.

Alex leaned in. "Man, I love you, too."

Ryan shook his head. He put his hand on Alex's shoulder, and Alex let him.

"No," Ryan said. "You don't get it, Alex. I mean... I *love* you, yeah? I'm *in love* with you. I have been for a while now."

You could've picked my jaw up off the floor. I knew it wasn't the time and place for me to be surprised by the admission, but I couldn't help it. As far as I'd known, Ryan had never been anything but straight. When I talked about my struggles as a bisexual woman, he never chimed in about similar struggles. I'd also never noticed the way he looked at Alex. I'd never seen the signs. It was strange, but somehow, that made me feel like a bad friend to both of them.

My gaze drifted back to the crimson surface of the water, checking for sirens. Nothing was there. My stomach lurched again, and I had to look away.

"Ryan," Alex said. "You... you're going through a lot right now. You don't know what you're saying."

"It's *because* I'm going through this that I'm saying it," he said.

Claire lowered her voice and leaned closer to me. "Should we be hearing this?"

"We don't have much of a choice," I replied. It wasn't like we could just walk off and give them privacy. Besides, Ryan didn't seem too bothered by us being there for this.

"You... do you mean it?" Alex asked. I noticed he'd backed away from Ryan, although he didn't look scared or disgusted, which was a good sign. I was pretty sure Alex was straight, but then again, I thought Ryan had been, too, and now he was proving me wrong.

"Of course I mean it," Ryan said. "Why the fuck else would I bring it up now?"

Alex took a deep breath. I could tell from the misty, far-off look in his eyes that he was not only trying not to cry but struggling to find the right words to convey whatever else he was feeling.

"Ryan," Alex said.

"We don't have to talk about it." Pink tinged Ryan's cheeks. I couldn't remember the last time I'd seen him or Alex embarrassed, or even at a loss for words.

"I'm... I don't think of you like that," Alex continued. "I mean, I'm... I'm flattered. It's an honor. But I don't feel that way

44

about you, or any other men. I'm sorry, you know. I wish..." He let his voice trail off.

"Don't do that," said Ryan. "Please don't give me hope. I know you never loved me—not like I love you. I've made my peace with it. I just... I just had to get it out. I had to tell you now. I wanted you to know before we—just in case."

What unspoken things had he meant to say to Ben? I couldn't imagine how badly that was weighing on him now. He'd never even had the chance to say goodbye to his baby brother.

"I know," Ryan said. "I know you don't love me back. I just needed you to know it. Do you understand?"

Alex sighed. He seemed to sink into himself. Then, he looked at me. I could read a decade of pain in that look, but maybe I was just projecting. He had to know how weird this all was for me, too. Ryan had been my first kiss. I'd lost my virginity to him. He'd been my first love. Despite all the shit that had happened between us, nothing could take those moments or memories away from us.

"In case something happens, I don't want to have any regrets," Ryan added.

My stomach twisted itself into a knot. The pain of losing Ben so suddenly and so traumatically burned through my veins and made my heart hurt. I pressed a hand against my chest like that could fix the problem.

"Thank you," Alex said. "For telling me, I mean."

Ryan only nodded. He put his face in his hands again, only if he cried again, I couldn't hear it. I couldn't imagine or even try to grasp what he was going through.

"It was fast," Claire said.

Alex frowned at her. "What was?"

"Ben," she continued. "It happened so quickly, he probably didn't feel it."

Ryan's head snapped up and drilled her with a scathing look. "If you think that for a minute, you're a fucking idiot. And, if you think that saying anything like that could help me feel better, you're a fucking asshole, too."

45

Claire swallowed. She closed her eyes and said nothing for a few minutes. The only sounds in the bunker were dripping water and Ryan's sniffling as he cried.

I pulled my knees to my chest and hugged them. If we didn't get out of there, we were fucked. I couldn't see a way out. Judging by the grim expressions on the others' faces, they didn't have any clue, either. That meant only one dark, inescapable truth.

We were going to die down there.

I wasn't ready to die yet. I regretted every dumb thing I'd ever done and every smart thing I hadn't. I regretted dropping out of film school, never confessing my feelings to Alex, not living up to my full creative potential. More than anything, I regretted agreeing to come down into this bunker in the first place.

I should've told Alex that I didn't want to do the job. But then, my group of friends would be dying here alone. Somehow that was worse to me than dying down here with them.

"We need to get out of here," I said.

"Stating the obvious," Claire deadpanned. I pressed my lips together, swallowed a snappy retort. We didn't have time to argue.

"If anyone has any ideas," I said, "I'm open to hearing them."

"I think we all are," Alex added.

Ryan sniffed again. "Maybe we aren't supposed to escape. Maybe we all have to die here with Ben."

I knew it had to be the grief talking, and Ryan had suffered an unthinkable loss, but Jesus Christ. That sentiment wasn't helping anyone.

"You know that's not true," I replied. "Ben wouldn't want us to just... give up."

"How do you know what Ben would want?" Ryan demanded. "He was my brother. Mine. He was my family. None of you can ever understand..."

His tirade dissolved into more pained crying. Once again, he hid his face from us. I watched his shoulders jerk with the effort of his sobs and wished that I could comfort him. There was nothing any one of us could do to help his pain, and I didn't think we could count on Ryan much for help.

"They popped the rafts," Alex said. "Those were our tickets out of here. We could try to swim, but based on—based on what we've seen, I don't think that's an option. They have a clear advantage."

I nodded and said, "I'm a good swimmer, but I don't think any of us stands a chance against them in the water, for incredibly obvious reasons."

Claire drummed her fingers against her knee. "We could keep going?"

Alex frowned at her. "Keep going where?"

"Further into the bunker?" I asked. "Is that what you're trying to say?"

"Think about it," Claire said. "You're right. We can't compete with them when it comes to swimming. But who says the way back is the only way out?"

"Old, busted-up place like this," I said. Realization dawned on me. "There's probably another exit. There almost has to be."

"So... what?" Alex asked, his frown softening. "We go deeper into the bunker and just... hope for the best?" He sighed. "That requires getting in the water again, and as we've already said, swimming spells death."

He had a point. The more I looked at the water, the worse I felt. It was dark and oppressive and God knew how deep. Besides that, the sirens waited for us. We couldn't go back the way we'd come.

But, what if we stole the sirens' attentions? What if we distracted them long enough to slip by them?

I lowered my voice so that Ryan wouldn't hear me—not that he was paying much attention to us at that point anyway. "When Ben was in the water thrashing around," I said, "that was all the sirens cared about."

"A diversion," Claire said. "We just need to figure out how to distract them."

"I'll do it," Alex said. "I volunteer as the distraction."

God, I didn't want this. I didn't want Alex to do this. Dread sank like a stone in the pit of my stomach, and tears pricked the backs of my eyes. Agreeing to this was essentially a death sentence. All of us knew that — especially Alex.

"Alex," I said. "You should think about this."

"I don't need to," he replied. "I've already decided. I'm the strongest swimmer, and it makes the most sense. You can't change my mind on this."

"Please don't do this," Ryan said. We all looked at him. It was the first sign he'd given that he was hearing anything we were saying. "Alex, as your best friend, I cannot let you do this."

"I want to," Alex said.

Harper rose out of the water, red hair plastered to her face. A slimy pink snake was draped around her neck and shoulders, and only when she pushed her chest out of the water did I see the kinks and turns and recognize that it was not a snake at all. It was Ben's intestines.

Harper grinned at us and said, "He tasted scared. The poor boy couldn't swim, could he?"

Alex hurried over to stand in front of Ryan so he couldn't see what Harper was wearing around her neck. Ryan leaned left and right to try to see around Alex, but Alex kept moving.

"It's for your own good," Alex said. "You've seen too much already."

I looked back at Harper. The sight of the intestines around her neck should have turned my stomach, but after all we'd been through so far, I took it in stride.

"You're a fucking monster," Claire told her. "All three of you are."

Harper's grin widened, her sharp teeth glinting red. Ryan crawled to the side and vomited then. He stayed on his knees at the edge of the water, holding his stomach like that alone could help him keep it together.

Alex's resolve never wavered. He lowered his voice, creeping close to Claire and me so that Harper wouldn't hear what he was saying. "I want to do this," he said. "Please, let me do this."

A memory from our childhood resurfaced. The four of us were still in elementary school. Alex, Ryan, and I were all part of the same class, and Ben was a few grades below us. One day on the playground, the teachers brought out popsicles for everyone. It was so hot they started melting as soon as we unwrapped them, and the sticky juice slid down our arms.

Alex and Ryan both wanted a red popsicle. There was only one left. Alex gave it to Ryan. I'd never forget it. Even at nine, he'd been selfless.

In the present, Claire and I exchanged a look. I could tell from how wet her eyes were that she was holding back tears, which meant she cared for Alex enough to want to cry. Maybe I could trust her after all.

I sighed, and it felt like losing a part of myself. "Only if you swear it's not a suicide attempt."

Sidney and Molly surfaced. Dread twisted my stomach in knots. The three sirens were close enough for me to touch them if I wanted.

Alex met my gaze and nodded. "I don't want to die," he said. "I'm willing to if it means helping y'all get out of here, but... but I mean, I don't want those bitches to tear me into pieces." He risked a look at Ryan. "Sorry."

Ryan waved him off. "You have to be careful. For me, if no one else."

"I will be," Alex answered.

My heart thudded painfully in my chest, threatening to punch through my ribcage. That would've been the perfect time for me to confess my feelings for Alex. Sure, it wasn't the private, perfect moment I'd envisioned, but if anything happened to him afterward, at least I'd feel a sense of closure.

I swallowed the lump in my throat. "Alex, I need to tell you something."

"Tell me later," he said.

"But you—"

"Later." His voice was firm, his expression resolute. "You'll see me after. Promise."

I could only nod.

Harper and the others circled the platform. I watched their tails as they cut through the water, feeling sick again.

Ryan crawled toward us on his hands and knees. "I have an idea. Liv, throw your camera."

I gaped at him. "What?"

"Just do it, okay?"

I didn't want to lose the camera, but we didn't have much choice. I picked up the camera, drew my arm back, and hurled the camera as far as I could. It plunged into the water with a splash.

The sirens stopped circling. Their tails cut through the water again as they took off in search of the disturbance.

"Throw yours, too, Claire," I said.

Claire grabbed her camera and chucked it toward the sirens. It landed farther away than mine had, making a bigger splash. Hopefully, investigating would keep the sirens busy.

"Thank you," Ryan said.

"We can get y'all new cameras," Alex said, though his words rang hollow.

"Don't worry about it," I said.

Ryan pulled Alex into a hug. Alex hesitated before kissing Ryan's cheek.

Ryan went scarlet. "I thought you said—"

"Just in case," Alex said. "I fucking love you, man. I love all of you."

"You promised," I said.

"And I intend to keep it." He took a deep breath, steeling himself for what he had to do next. "Wish me luck, all right?"

Before any of us could stop him, he lowered himself into the water and started swimming out toward where we'd seen the sirens.

With Alex in the water, we had to move quickly. There was no telling how much time he could buy us. I grabbed Ryan's hand and pulled him into the water with me. If he tried to protest, I was prepared to argue, but he didn't say a word, and he kept holding onto my hand.

Claire slipped into the water next to us and took my other hand. I let her.

Alex started thrashing around in the water, trying to draw the sirens' attention. We were in the water now, but since none of us were bleeding — and we weren't moving much — I hoped we looked much less appealing than he did. He probably hoped that, too.

"Hey!" Alex shouted. "Hey, you bitches! Come and get me! Hot, fresh food right here!"

"Jesus," Ryan hissed.

I squeezed his hand. "We have to go, Ryan. He's doing this for us. We need to trust him."

Harper drifted toward Alex like she had all the time in the world. For a minute, I didn't see the others, and I worried the plan wouldn't work. Then, Molly and Sidney's heads broke the surface of the water, and they made a beeline for Alex. My stomach clenched, but I reminded myself that this was all part of the plan. This was what we'd wanted to happen. As terrible as it felt, we'd have to persevere.

We were going to be okay. The sirens weren't even looking at us. We could do this.

Maybe it wouldn't be too long before we made it out of the bunker altogether.

I pulled Ryan and Claire along as silently as I could, swimming toward the closest wall. It was hard to tell from the shitty lighting, but I thought I could see a crack in the wall. It had to lead somewhere.

Although I couldn't see any light coming through from the other side, maybe it could be a room that opened up into a way out somehow. We just had to make it through. At any rate, it had to be better than staying out in the open with the sirens.

"I think we can fit through there," I whispered once we got closer. I didn't even want to think about what Alex was doing out there or what could be happening to him. I assumed he was still thrashing, still swimming around. And since I didn't hear any screaming, he had to be okay, right?

That's what I had to tell myself.

I got my shoulder against the wall, right beside the crack, when Alex finally cried out.

Ryan let go of my hand right away. Zero hesitation. I knew he was going back for Alex without even having to ask him. It was something I would've done, too, had Alex not reassured us that this would be part of the plan — a plan that Ryan was now very much putting in jeopardy by acting on impulse.

Claire and I switched places. She let go of my hand and stared at me, wide-eyed.

"What?" I asked.

"Aren't you going to go after him?" she answered.

In another world, I might've rolled my eyes at her. But, at this point, I was barely even holding it together myself. I did think it was a terrible idea for Ryan to do what he was doing, but there was no point in saying, "I told you so" if he was dead. Claire had a point. If I didn't want to lose another friend—or two of them— I'd have to intervene.

"Don't move," I said to Claire. "I'll be right back."

Before I could second-guess myself, I started in Ryan's direction. Molly's black head popped out of the water and lunged toward Ryan. She grabbed him. She tore his arm off, spilling more blood into the water, and he screamed.

"Fuck!" I said. "Claire, we need—"

"Ryan!" Alex shouted. He pivoted and swam toward Ryan, which distracted Molly enough that she let go of him. Claire swam up beside me, and together with Alex, we grabbed Ryan. We managed to haul him off and over to the crack, swimming as fast as we could to outrace the sirens.

Even more blood bloomed in the water around Ryan. The sirens still had him.

Molly pulled his leg off, and the cloud of blood in the water seemed to explode in a way I hadn't seen before. I think the bleeding came from an artery in his leg — the femoral artery.

Claire, Alex, and I ducked through the crack in the bunker wall. We could still hear Ryan screaming. I'll never forget that sound.

Someone had left an old plane in the space behind the crack. Before any of the sirens could slip through the crack and get us, Claire and I grabbed the plane and pushed it up against the entrance, sealing it with a wing. We didn't have anything heavier to wedge against it, so it would have to do for the time being. As it was, we were all too shaken up to think further ahead, anyway. All that mattered then was that we three were safe.

The space behind the crack was bigger than I'd expected. It was a huge room that felt cave-like, with a pinprick of light coming in at the top and water lapping at a makeshift shore. In addition to the plane, there was a pile of discarded parts and metal, a dilapidated desk piled high with papers, a rusted file cabinet, and a safe with the door wide open. I couldn't see anything inside. It looked like its contents had already been plundered God knows how many years ago.

We collapsed on the shoreline, utterly depleted. The concrete was hard and cold under my ass, but I barely felt the discomfort. My insides felt like they'd been scooped out and replaced with a sharp, aching numbness.

Grief is funny. It teaches you things about yourself you otherwise wouldn't have noticed. For me, I learned that numbness doesn't equal nothingness; that emptiness isn't the absence of pain. In the wake of losing Ben, I'd felt a trickle of it. After losing Ryan, I felt the whole damn river.

I'm not sure how long I cried. I only know that I did, putting my face in my hands and bawling until I felt like I couldn't breathe, like I didn't even exist anymore.

That was when I realized we might not make it out alive. Not one of us. Until that point, I'd held out hope that maybe we could do it, but after losing two of my friends in the span of a day, it didn't seem likely we could avoid a similar fate.

If Claire realized this, too, she didn't show it. She comforted herself by hugging her knees to her chest and staring straight ahead like the key to our future was out there somewhere.

Alex sat still, too. He had his legs stretched out in front of him and his hands resting in his lap. He turned his palms up and looked down at them. I'd never seen his face look so hard before.

"I'm so tired," he murmured. "I'm so sick of losing friends."

"We should rest," I said. I didn't know what else to say. There were certainly no words to make what had happened any better, nothing I could do to help alleviate the pain we all were feeling at that moment.

"I don't want to rest," Alex said. "I want to get the fuck out of this place."

I understood that. Of course I did. Mostly because I felt the same way. But we weren't thinking clearly — especially Alex — and we needed to be in the best possible frame of mind if we could ever hope to try to figure out how to get out of there. I knew Alex so well I could almost tell what he was thinking. Claire, I was less sure of. Whatever it took, we needed to present a united front if we wanted to stand a chance of getting out of outwitting the sirens once and for all and getting out of the bunker alive.

My best shot at figuring out how to get out was to make a plan with Claire. If Alex participated, too, that would be ideal, but I knew better than to expect that from him now. He wasn't exactly in his right mind. Claire and I weren't, either, but we were better off than him—or, at least, it seemed that way.

"Alex," I said gently, "lie down and try to rest. One of us can wake you in an hour."

Alex looked at me, but almost all the fight had left his eyes. He nodded meekly, stretching out on the cold cement and shutting his eyes. I don't know if he was planning to go to sleep. All I knew was that we had to do our best to figure out a way out or we were doomed.

The worst thing about our fates in the bunker was the idea that no one would find us. No one would know what had happened to us. I thought back to the pile of bones with the teeth marks on them, to the water bottle. If we didn't make it out, we would be nothing but a memory, with no real evidence of what hell we'd gone through down here.

Ben and Ryan's family would already suffer, but they didn't need to suffer more. We could make it out of there. We didn't even have their sons' bodies.

I swallowed the lump in my throat. We had to focus on finding our way out of this bunker.

"Claire," I murmured. I kept my voice low, in case Alex dozed off. I was also quiet because I didn't want him to get paranoid that we were planning something without him. He was on the edge of insanity. The last thing we needed was him thinking we were against him, too.

Claire looked at me. Her eyelashes were wet, though whether from the water or from crying, I couldn't be sure. Mine had to be, too.

"Over there," she said, pointing to the desk and all the wreckage around it. "We can be quieter there. You know, just in case."

I knew neither of us wanted to consider the possibility that the sirens would come through the crack in the wall somehow. If we made too much noise, it felt like giving ourselves away somehow, even though they knew we were already in here. It felt like giving up.

I chanced another look at Alex before heading over to the far wall with Claire. We sat on the cold floor, stretching our legs out in front of us. We weren't far enough from Alex to not be overheard, but if he wanted to sleep, I was confident that he could tune us out.

I thought back to the last real conversation I'd had with

Claire. How she'd grown up in the haunted house and no one had believed her. I believed her, even now. Especially with all we'd been through together so far.

"We need to figure out what to do," she whispered.

"Understatement of the century," I said. "We already know what we need to do, yeah? We need to get the fuck out of this bunker."

"Easier said than done." Claire looked down at her legs, frowning. "It's only a matter of time before we either starve to death or risk heading out there and letting them catch us. We don't stand a chance against them in the water."

I ran a hand down my face. "We don't have much choice."

"I know that, too. We at least need to try."

I sighed. It felt so impossible. I wished we'd never gone down there. I wished I'd never even answered Alex's text. It was too late for regrets.

"We need to work through this thing together," Claire said. "You and me, I mean."

"I agree," I said. "Alex isn't going to be much help to us right now."

Claire closed her eyes. "I wish I hadn't lost the camera. You don't happen to still have yours with you, do you?"

"Afraid not."

"I figured. Still, would've been nice."

"It's gonna be hard to get anyone to believe us after this. No bodies, no footage, no real proof of what we've seen. What we've experienced."

"I know. It sucks."

"I only have one idea for getting us out here. I don't think you'll like it, either, but it's the only chance we've got."

"Spill it, sister."

"What if... God, this sounds so fucking wild, but what if we try to appeal to the sirens, woman to woman? Or... human women to feminine monsters or whatever the fuck they are."

The furrow between Claire's eyebrows deepened, and her lips

turned downward in a scowl. "What, like a 'bitches against the patriarchy' type thing?"

"Think about it," I said. "If we just try to get them to see us as humans first, it won't work. They can't relate to us. I know we've been working off the assumption that they were all humans, too, once — that's what they told us — but what if they're not? I think it's far more likely they've never been human. But they look feminine, right?"

"I guess so," Claire said. She looked away, staring out at the water. "You want us to stake our lives on the idea that sirens deal with patriarchal bullshit in their society, too?"

"Unless you've got a better idea, yeah, I do," I answered.

"Look, I'm not completely against it. It's no less whacko than the other shit we've done."

"I know this is messy," I said. "And I wish we had time to put together something more polished, but obviously, we don't." I leaned my head against the wall. "But if we can appeal to them on any level, this might be the only way."

"Fine, okay," Claire said. "You win. Let's give it a shot."

Claire used the wall to push herself to a standing position and brushed off the back of her pants. It seemed like such a normal gesture that it made me want to cry. I looked back at Alex, who appeared to be fast asleep. Either that, or he was doing the world's best job of pretending. His mouth had dropped open and every-thing. I wasn't sure how good his quality of sleep could be, but if one of us could get even five minutes of peace, it had to be better than nothing.

"Don't move," I told Alex, knowing he couldn't hear me. I had so much more to say to him, and I hated to wait until we got back, but I didn't have any choice anymore.

ANDIE

A month after meeting Liv, I was spending more time with her than my wife. With me putting in long hours at the station for this case, Joy and I were even more like ships in the night than usual. When I was home, I was either eating, sleeping, or thinking about Liv and her story. Whenever Liv needed a break from her story, I'd bring her coffee or water, and we'd talk about our lives. On a few occasions, we'd even managed to make each other laugh.

Liv was gorgeous when she smiled. This observation only made my heart hurt worse for her.

Dad's office was sweltering when I walked in. Like the rest of the precinct, it didn't have any air-conditioning at the time. A small metal fan from the 1960s whirred on the edge of his desk.

"Hot for November," I said.

"It's Georgia," he replied.

The chief himself sat in his enormous chair with a paper fan in hand, waving it at his face. He tugged at his collar as I entered. This time, he didn't stand.

"Sergeant," he said, "why don't you have a seat."

It wasn't a question. I kept my hand on the half-open door.

"Please," he added.

The politeness meant he didn't want to have this conversation. Reluctantly, I shut the door behind me and stepped further into the room. Normally, Dad would've stood for me. I don't know whether the heat or his hesitation toward me was to blame for him remaining seated this time. Nevertheless, he didn't stand, and he didn't shake my hand or even clap me on the shoulder. Feeling more and more like a little boy being scolded, I sank into the metal folding chair in front of his desk. I took off my hat and set it in my lap, running a hand through my hair.

"Dad," I began.

He raised a hand to stop me. "Andie, I'm not just your dad. I'm your boss."

Fuck. It was going to be one of *those* talks.

I swallowed. "If this is about the Reyes case—"

"It is," he said. "But humor me first. Sergeant... I never should've put you on this case. I see that now." He sighed. "That day when you walked in the station, when I said you were reassigned, I saw your face fall. That was when I realized I'd made a mistake."

"But you didn't make a mistake," I said. "That other case... that case was just like every other case I've handled."

"That's my point. Look, for as long as you've been on the force, we've never had any problems, you and me. Most of the folks around here would say the same." He leaned back in his chair, put his hands together, and steepled his fingers. "You're a hell of a cop, Andie. Dependable, and passionate. But that passion might get you in trouble."

"If I'm here, that means it has," I said.

I'd handled the Reyes case by the book. As strange as it was, no one could deny that.

So far, I'd formed a bond with Liv. I'd gotten her to trust us and to open up, to tell us things she might not have told any other officers here. She trusted me.

When I'd spoken to Claire's parents, I'd even managed that without falling all over myself. Honestly and objectively, I couldn't understand what I'd done wrong. Not one single thing.

But, if the chief had called me into his office at the beginning of a shift like this, I must have done something out of pocket.

"With all due respect," he said.

"Whenever people say that it means they're about to say something disrespectful," I said, shaking my head. "If you have something bad to say to me, say it. I don't want to waste time dancing around whatever this is."

He ran his tongue over his teeth. For a minute, I worried I'd pushed him too hard. Instead, he looked at me with something like respect as he launched into what he'd brought me in to say. "I'm taking you off the Reyes case. You're too attached. I need someone more objective."

I pounded my fist on the desk. "You can't!"

"I absolutely can," he replied. "And I am. I'm your *boss*, Sergeant McCollum. You need to calm down."

Calm down. A minute ago, he'd admired my passion.

"Officer Lyle isn't experienced enough for this," I pleaded. It was a lousy excuse, but it was the most objective thing I could come up with in the heat of the moment. He'd cornered me. "She... she needs more time before she can handle something like this on her own."

"I'll put someone else on it with her." He quirked an eyebrow at me. "Is this going to escalate, or can we talk like two adults?"

Rage simmered under my skin, but I nodded. I wouldn't get what I wanted if he thought I was just being insolent. "Sir."

"I also didn't ask you for feedback on your partner, just so we're clear." He shook his head. "I don't know what's gotten into you, and it worries the hell out of me. Your behavior toward Miss Reyes—"

"Liv insisted I call her by her first name. I was only trying—"

"Let me *finish*, Andie. Shit." He leaned back in his chair, shaking his head again. "This is exactly what I'm talking about. That attitude. That's not something you would've showcased before this assignment. That's why I want to take you off this case."

My pulse was pounding in my ears. I had to bite my tongue to keep from firing off a retort that might've gotten me suspended. Joy's job didn't bring in enough money for the both of us. As much as I hated to say it, I was the breadwinner. I had to keep this job or both of us were screwed. At that moment, I was glad our child hadn't made it or there'd be another mouth to feed—and I felt a pang of guilt for ever having thought that.

"If you take me off the case, what happens to her?" I asked.

"Miss Reyes will be well taken care of," Dad assured me. "We can keep Officer Lyle assigned to her for consistency, and I'll let you help me choose your replacement."

"Replacement," I repeated. Was he firing me?

"For the case," he clarified. "Trust me, you're not going anywhere."

I worked my jaw as I considered what the fuck he was saying. Why did he think he had to take me off the case? What the fuck did that mean, that I'd gotten too attached? Didn't he want me to be invested in my cases?

"I don't understand," I answered honestly.

"You don't have to understand. You just have to comply," he said.

It was the same song and dance I'd gotten for my whole life in this town. The rules didn't need to make sense. They were the rules. They were there for you to follow, not to question. For most of my life, I'd fallen in line. Hell, I'd been so happy to follow the rules that I'd pledged myself to protect and enforce them. Wasn't that what I should've been doing here? Why was the chief getting in my way?

"What?" Dad demanded. "What are you looking at me like that for?"

I shook my head, sighing. "I don't want to do this."

"No one said anything about what you want. Do you think I want to sit in here and have this kind of talk with you? Hell no. I have about a million other things to do, and more pressing reassignments to deliver."

"Then what am I doing here?"

"Your partner complained."

"Who cares? This isn't about my partner."

"First of all, I care. Second, you're right, but I can't just disregard her." He ran his hand over the top of his head. "She's... she's worried about what's best for Miss Reyes, that's all."

"Bullshit," I said. It came out more loudly than I'd intended, but there was no going back now. "If she was concerned about doing the best thing for Liv, she'd want to keep me on the case. We've developed a rapport. She trusts me."

"That's the problem," Dad said. He laid his hands flat on the desk, palms facing down. "You're Icarus flying too close to the sun, to rehash an over-hashed analogy. This level of attachment isn't good for anyone." He paused. "I hate to ask this, but... do you have a crush on her?"

I bristled, even though I couldn't deny it. "Doesn't matter."

He sighed. "You're a married woman, Andie."

"Maybe not for long."

His face softened first, then his voice. "Is it the job?"

I wasn't sure what the most honest way to answer that one was. There was a big picture window behind the chief's head, so I redirected my gaze to the setting outside it.

"Been a long time coming, but meeting Liv helped."

"See, the more I hear things like that coming from you, the more convinced I am that this is the right thing. That I'm making the right decision."

"You can't take me off the case. Please, Dad."

"I wish there were another way, but you know I can't play favorites — or even look like I might play favorites."

"I'll—I'll try something else," I said. "A different approach. I'll back off, okay?"

"What's that supposed to mean?" Dad asked.

"What if I let Lyle handle most of the questioning that's left?" I said. "I'll hang back a little more, like she's been doing. That way, Liv — Miss Reyes — can talk to her instead of me."

"Hm. It could work," Dad said. "Of course, there's the chance she'd just ask to talk to you, anyway."

"Well, yeah. I can't do anything about that, though. I can hardly be blamed for Miss Reyes's decisions."

"No, Andie. I suppose you can't."

"Where does that leave us, then?"

"Not far from where we started," Dad said. "Look, if I had my way, I never would've even pulled you into my office for this. Seems like a massive waste of time as well as energy. I've got parents calling in about missing kids and this girl claiming she's seen killer mermaids, and you're the only one around here who can make heads or tails of any of it. I'd prefer to keep you on the case, but I need to know that I can trust you."

"You can trust me, Chief," I said. "You know that."

"So, you'll back off?" Dad asked.

"Yes," I said. "I'll let Lyle take the lead. I can be... less familiar."

"And, if Miss Reyes engages you in conversation, don't be cold," Dad said. "Just don't be pulling overtime or overnight shifts or anything. We can't afford to botch this one with the GBI breathing down our necks."

"I know, Chief."

"Thank you," Dad said. "And hey, Andie?"

"Yeah?"

"Don't make me regret this."

I nodded. The pressure was on me to do a good job with this case, to prove that I could handle even bigger and better cases. The opportunity had been a long time coming. I wasn't wasting it. When I got back to the interview room, Liv had her head down on the table. Her eyes were closed. At first, I thought she might be sleeping.

"Sergeant," she said.

I sat in the chair across the table from her. "Are you ready to get back into it?"

"No, but I figure that's why you're here."

I felt for her. I really did. She'd been through hell — I knew at least that much, even if I didn't know the full extent of it yet. From her appearance alone, I could tell I was in for the interview of a lifetime.

"The sooner we get through this, the sooner we can let you go," I said. Immediately, I regretted my choice of words. "Not that we're detaining you or anything, of course. You're free to come and go as you please."

She raised her head and smirked. "I know, sergeant."

Of course she did. She'd *been* coming and going. I needed to pull it together.

"Are you ready?" I asked her.

"Yeah," she said. "I'll play."

LIV

Claire and I napped in shifts. I can't speak for her, but I slept like hell. I wasn't even sure I'd drifted off to sleep. One minute, I was wide awake; the next, Claire was shaking my shoulder and telling me it was her turn.

We still hadn't woken Alex. In the grand scheme of our plotting, I doubted he could help. Besides, if he was going to be of any help to the two of us later, we needed him rested — more so than he'd been when we arrived.

Reluctantly, I let Claire sleep. She deserved the rest. Still, I couldn't help feeling we had no idea what we were up against. I wanted to get back to the surface alive, and I was willing to do just about anything I could to make that happen, and I wanted to talk it through with Claire.

I'd been turning our plan over in my head, trying to make sure it felt solid enough to pursue. Then again, even if we didn't, did we have any other choice? The only other idea I could even entertain was to our way out with brute force. We didn't have any weapons, and we didn't stand a chance against the sirens in the water. I wasn't even sure that there was any way to hurt them, let alone kill them.

Unless we beat the sirens at their own game.

I wasn't sure how much time had passed before Claire was

conscious again, or what had even woken her. She sat up, rubbing her eyes with her fists. When I met her gaze, she yawned and asked, "How are we doing this?"

I dragged my bottom lip through my teeth. We hadn't exactly nailed down the specifics of what we wanted to say to the sirens, how we wanted to try to appeal to them.

"We don't even know they're still out there," I said. "But if they are, we need to be careful."

"Harper's their leader," Claire said. "We need to get her on our side."

"Sure," I agreed. "So, we get Harper to trust us. We get her to see us in a sympathetic light. If we can manage that, we're set."

Claire nodded. "I'm behind you, okay? No matter what happens."

Together, the two of us walked into the water. I felt my heartbeat in my stomach. After carefully moving the plane aside, we swam up to the wall. Hopefully, someone was waiting outside.

"Harper," I called.

The siren appeared. The splash as she broke the surface of the water was closer than I wanted it to be.

I swam over to the crack and put my face through it, still clinging to the plane.

"Harper," I said. "You're Harper, tight?"

She nodded. I tried not to linger on the blood that streaked her mouth—Ben's blood, or Ryan's. Maybe both. The less I remembered how monstrous the trio was, the better.

"Harper, I have a family," I said. "A pretty big family, even by human standards." I paused, waiting to see if Claire would join in. She didn't. "Lots of siblings. I don't know how siren families work, but I know you have sisters, too. I'm guessing you love them."

"Yes," Harper offered.

"My family is big, and so many of them get on my nerves, but I'd do almost anything for them if they asked me." I paused, searching for the right words. "You and your sisters are close. I'm sure there's very little that you wouldn't do for them."

Harper nodded. Claire nudged me, but I wasn't sure whether she thought I should stop or if she was encouraging me. I assumed the latter and I kept going. Nothing ventured, nothing gained.

"I can understand why you're doing what you're doing," I said. "You want to take care of your sisters. That's it, isn't it?" Again, Harper nodded. "I would do anything for my family, too," I went on. "I want to make them happy. That's why I need to make it out of this bunker. You understand that, right?"

Her eyes narrowed. "I can't just... let you leave. How would I feed my sisters?"

I hesitated. This wasn't going how I'd wanted, and I didn't see any other way forward. I glanced over at Claire. She was frowning.

"What if we bring you more people," I said, ignoring the look Claire shot me. "What if... if you let us get out of here, and we bring you a steady supply of food for years to come." I paused. "For as long as we live, if you want."

Harper raised her eyebrows. "You would do that?"

"I'd be willing to, yes. That's how badly I want to get back to my family."

I looked back at Claire, desperately needing her to help out with this pitch. I was doing all I could to sell it, but if she didn't throw her enthusiasm in, too, I didn't think we stood a chance of swaying Harper.

Harper looked at Claire, too. She wanted both of our cooperation.

Claire cleared her throat and swallowed. "Sidney and... and Molly," she said. "They just want food, right? That's all you three want from us. We can provide that. It's like a one-for-one trade. And we'll keep bringing food to you. That's got to be worth something."

Harper's eyes narrowed as she considered our proposition. This was my last-ditch effort to get the two of us—three, counting Alex, still sleeping—out of the bunker. Out into the light of day and the relative safety of the world beyond. If this didn't work, we were fucked.

"I should talk to them first," Harper said.

"No," Claire jumped in, a little too quickly. Shit, she was showing our hand.

I glanced back toward the crack in the wall. I thought about Alex. It helped.

"You're their leader, aren't you?" I said, trying to smooth things over. If Claire cost us our shot, I would never forgive her — not that I'd live long enough to do that, anyway. "Don't they trust you to make this decision?"

Harper's frown lifted. "You have a valid point. They've... their patience with me has been thin, anyway." Her tail swished in the water. "So, you two want out of here?"

"There's three of us," I said. *Three of us left.*

Harper pulled a strand of hair over her shoulder and twirled it in her hand, considering. I felt like all the air had been sucked out of the bunker.

"Okay," Harper said. "I'll... let you out, as long as you promise to bring more people back for me. And you have to let me escort you out of the bunker—as far as I can go in the water, anyway." She paused. "Do we have a deal?"

Relieved tears pricked my eyes. I couldn't believe it. I couldn't believe we'd gotten through to her. I'd carried out our plan and it worked. We were getting out.

"We need to go back and get Alex," Claire said.

"The... man?" Harper frowned again. "I didn't agree to the man leaving here. The men in your group are loud, are they not? They're strong. *Meaty.*"

I paled and hoped to God she didn't notice it. I could all but feel Claire glaring daggers at Harper, but I wasn't about to let her ruin this opportunity for us. It wasn't that I wanted to leave Alex behind. It wasn't even that I thought we had to. But, at that moment, for us to make it out of that bunker alive, I needed Harper to think we were willing to cut him loose.

"If Alex will sweeten the pot," I said, "we're happy to leave him behind."

Claire's hatred for me radiated off her in waves. She glared at me, and I wished I could've told her that I didn't mean it..

"Right," said Harper. "Anyway, if you two come with me, I can get you out. But it has to be the two of you. Forget the man. You're not getting him back."

"So, you're saying you won't eat us?" I reiterated. Harper hadn't shown any outward aggression since we'd gotten there, but I had to make sure. If something happened to me—or worse, to Claire and me—then Alex would be alone. And, based on the shaky state we'd left him in, he couldn't to get himself out of this hole.

Harper's gaze slid over Claire, lingering on her face, before drifting back to me. I forced a smile, and she smiled back, serrated teeth gleaming in the scant light coming in. I held back a shiver.

"We have a deal," Harper said. "I won't kill you. You can trust me."

All the tension in my body left, and I sighed. We had done it. I felt like throwing my arms around her, but we weren't out of there just yet. We had a long way still to go. Later, we could celebrate. For now, we had to keep going.

"Follow me," Harper said.

I exchanged a look with Claire. This close to Harper, we couldn't say a word without her overhearing, but I tried to convey with my eyes that this was going to be okay. We'd gotten Harper to go along with our scheme for now. We were getting out of there, come hell or high water — or sirens.

"There's another air pocket," Harper said. "You have to dive a bit, and swim to get there. When you surface, you'll see the sky. That's what you both want, yes?"

"Yes," I breathed. I didn't trust myself to say much else beyond that. Hope swelled in my gut, and it was so overpowering, I felt like I might puke.

We were getting out of there.

"Can you swim well?" I asked Claire. I'd seen her swim earlier, of course, but that was a life-or-death situation. She might have been running on instinct or adrenaline. I didn't know if she was prepared for whatever might come next.

"I could do a goddamn backflip if it would get us out," she said.

"Me, too," I agreed. "Let's do this."

Harper's head dipped beneath the water. I held my breath and followed. The water was clear enough for me to make out Harper's silhouette, but it wasn't easy to see where she was going. Claire's hand slipped into mine. I tugged her after me, hurrying to catch up with Harper. We squeezed through a flooded tunnel with no air pockets and I worried we'd be goners, but then Harper swam up and disappeared from view. She floated above us, her head above water.

I broke the surface and gasped. Fresh air poured into my lungs. Instead of a skylight above us, the bunker opened up to more sky than I thought existed in our subterranean prison. I swore I could even hear noise from outside.

Tears stung my eyes again.

"We did it, Claire. We made it. We're getting out of here," I said.

We could come back to the bunker for Alex. We could recover Ben's and Ryan's bodies, too — or whatever was left of them. I couldn't help thinking back to the bones, covered in teeth marks and all.

Ben and Ryan's family deserved something to bury, some closure. I was already thinking of everything I'd do once I got home. I thought about going to the military, convincing them to come in. The bunker belonged to them; we were trespassers. Maybe they'd be eager to enforce those restrictions. They could bring in tanks or bombs, maybe heavy artillery—something massive to wipe out the sirens and stop them from hurting or killing anyone else.

As soon as we got out of there, everything would be all right.

The corners of my mouth lifted. As my eyes scanned the walls, though, my body went rigid.

There were no doors there. No seams. It was water and walls and sky we couldn't reach.

Harper had lied to us.

Claire gripped my arm. Her voice shook. "What the fuck is going on?"

"It's a trap," I said, trying to keep my voice calm. "Harper... Harper knew this wasn't an exit. Her sisters are probably on their way now."

"Shit." Claire let go of my arm, whirling around to look at Harper. Only, she wasn't there anymore. "Oh, fuck. Now we don't even know where she is, do we?"

"No."

It wasn't looking good for us, let alone Alex. For all we knew, the sirens had gotten him already. Maybe Harper had lured us out so the others could attack him.

A tail swished in the water. By the time I spun around to see whose it was, the siren wrapped her hand around my arm. Fiery eyes burned into mine: Molly.

I screamed. Molly tried to drag me into the water. I pulled and twisted in her grip. I couldn't see Claire anymore. I shouted for her. "Claire! Claire, where the hell are you?"

I shouldn't have asked that, and immediately regretted it. If she answered me she would have given up her location, making it easier for Sidney or Harper to get her.

Molly put her hand on my other arm, jerking me toward her. Her smile was wide, showcasing her razor-sharp teeth. She raised her tail — almost too late, I remembered the barbs — and I dodged it in the nick of time, somehow rolling out of her grip.

Shit. I didn't know how we'd get out of this one.

"Claire!" I yelled again.

Molly hissed something in a language I didn't understand and lunged at me again, but I was too far back on the platform now for her to get to me. She dove under and swam to the other side. There was still a chance she'd ambush me.

A head broke the surface of the water on my right. I screamed.

Claire's face came into view instead, although an angry red slash crossed it.

"Jesus," I said.

"Sidney," Claire gasped. "Sidney—she got me, but then... I got away, I don't think—"

Someone—most likely Molly—pulled her back under. I reared back from the edge of the platform, but threw myself off balance. I toppled back on my ass. One of the sirens grabbed my hair and pulled me backward off the platform. It was Sidney, her dark eyes voids I didn't want to dissolve in. Her teeth were the sharpest of all of them, and the scariest. When she smiled at me, I thought for sure I was a goner.

Claire's head popped into view again. "Liv!"

"Claire!" I shrieked, kicking hard at Sidney. "Claire, we have—"

Sidney pulled me under. Air trailed in a steady stream of bubbles from my mouth, billowing around me as I fought to break free. I struggled against Sidney, guided by the light in her forehead. The water slowed my movements. When I went to kick her, it didn't do anything. Finally, she grabbed my arm, and I turned my head and bit her hard. I didn't let up even when I tasted blood.

Sidney roared in pain, a strange sound distorted by the water, and let go of me. I pushed off the side of the bunker and shot back up on the other side of the platform, near where we'd come in.

When my head broke the surface, I looked around for Claire, but I didn't see her. *Fuck*. A wave of dread and grief big enough to drown in almost knocked me over, but I had to keep going. If I didn't escape, they were going to get Alex. Worse, if I didn't make it, maybe no one would stop them. Maybe they'd keep killing people like this.

The burden of guilt for that possibility was one I couldn't shoulder.

The water around me warmed, and I noticed a lot of blood. Claire's head popped back out, and she let out a scream. I'll never forget how it echoed.

I knew I couldn't save her, but... I didn't even try. I used the feeding frenzy to get the fuck away, to get back to the hideout as soon as I could.

Out of everyone who died in there, Claire's death haunts me most.

ANDIE

"She didn't have to die," Liv said. "I came so close to saving her."

She sniffled, and I looked up from my notes. Tears streamed down her cheeks. I had no clue how long she'd been crying.

Lyle got up, her chair scraping the floor. "I'll go get some tissues."

I barely registered her leaving the room. I was too focused on Liv. How could I have been so shitty not to notice she was hurting? How could I have missed the minute she started crying?

"I'm so sorry," I said.

She waved me off. "It's okay."

"It's *not* okay. It's..." Before I could think about what I was doing, I clasped her hand between mine. She didn't pull back. "You've been through a hell of a lot, Liv. Most people in your position wouldn't be able to string two words together, let alone a whole statement. You're not only doing your best. You're blowing this out of the water." I winced. "Pun unintended."

Liv kept her eyes on mine. She squeezed my hand. "Thank you so much, Sergeant."

"Andie," I corrected her. "Please, Liv. You've earned that much from me, at least."

Joy had never looked at me the way Liv did at that moment: like I was the only shred of sanity she had, the anchor tethering her to the earth. I devoured that feeling. I wanted more of it. I wanted to be everything Liv needed me to be.

That's when I realized the chief had been right.

I was in over my head, and there was no escaping.

Liv squeezed my fingers. Her eyes went wide, but she didn't pull her hand back. Nor did she return what had to be my longing look with any of her own, though.

"What happens when I'm out of here?" she asked. Her voice was low and soft.

I knew what she was asking, as well as what she wasn't. But I couldn't exactly come right out and tell her that I understood. If I was wrong — as much as I doubted I could be — I'd get both of us in trouble.

"Do they have you staying somewhere?" I asked, even though I already knew the answer. Changing the subject was easier than lying.

"Hotel on Fifth," she said. "Protective custody, officers escorting me to and from. They think I'll hurt myself or I'll leave town or something. But you know that." Her eyes narrowed, and for the first time in a long time, it felt like we were back to square one. "What aren't you telling me, Andie?"

"You asked me what happens to you after this," I said. "The short answer is... I don't know. I've never handled a case like yours before. Once you've given me the rest of your account, I'll write up an incident report, and maybe I can get them to fast-track my request to investigate further." I paused. Her eyes weren't so narrow anymore, but they were still sharp, taking me in. "I want to go look for the sirens."

"*No.*" Liv's voice was so low, I almost didn't hear it. "You can't. No one can go down there."

I frowned. "Liv... until we investigate — and ultimately verify — the claims you're making, you'll be the prime suspect. You have to know that."

Her thick brows knitted together. "Suspect? For what?"

I paused. Jesus, of course they hadn't told her. I probably shouldn't have said anything, but it was too late to take it back. I didn't think that Liv would just let something like that slide.

"This won't surprise you, but Claire's moms have been here. Other parents, too." I swallowed. "I can't switch their cases from missing persons to homicides without proof. I believe you, Liv. Wholeheartedly. As crazy as it sounds, I can tell you're sincere. You believe you saw killer mermaids."

Okay, maybe *killer mermaids* had been glib, but I kept moving. No time to stop.

"That's where my request to investigate comes in," I continued. "If I can get enough relevant information from you to put in for a warrant, we're golden. I'll bring it to the chief, he'll sign off on it, and my team will search the park."

"You *can't*." Her voice was plaintive. Her fingers, still holding mine, tightened until I met her gaze. "Promise me, Andie, you won't go down there."

If I made that promise, I knew I wouldn't keep it. She knew I *couldn't* keep it.

Still, I said, "I promise.

J oy was in the bathtub when I got home. We hadn't said much to each other since the argument on Monday. It wasn't like we'd never disagreed before — this time, it was more about the things we hadn't said than the things we had.

I'm not happy, I hadn't said.

Neither am I, she hadn't replied.

I followed the glow of the bathroom light down the hallway. We had a nice tub in the master, but it wasn't big enough for Joy to stretch out in. Her brothers all played basketball, and she was just as tall. If she wanted to extend her legs and relax, she had to opt for the garden tub in the hall bathroom. The toilet in that one was broken. She'd asked me to get it fixed months ago, and I only remembered when I saw the cracked bowl again.

Joy's blonde head poked out over a tide of bubbles. Candles circled the tub, enveloping the room in a cornucopia of scents. She hadn't turned the overhead light on, but there were enough candles that to make the room look that bright.

"Hey," I said softly, leaning against the sink.

Joy didn't even turn her head.

"I can make dinner. Is chicken okay?"

Still, she didn't answer. Frustration squeezed my chest, made my voice catch.

"Jesus Christ, Joy. We can't do this forever."

She swiveled her head toward me. She wore a mask of neutrality. I hated when I couldn't figure out what she was thinking.

"You're talking in your sleep again," Joy said.

"What does that have to do with our current situation?"

"You were saying someone's name," she sighed. "I should've known. Who's Liv?"

All the frustration in my body turned to fear, and that fear trickled down into my stomach. I felt like puking.

"What did you say?" I asked.

"Andie." She cast a long, withering look at me before ducking her head underwater. I waited, arms crossed, for her to resurface. She was giving me the time to let her words sink in. She thought I hadn't heard her, but I had. That was the problem. When she came up and caught a breath, I leveled my gaze at her. It was the first time we'd looked each other in the eye since I got home.

"Liv is... a case," I said. "You have to trust me, Joy. Have I ever betrayed your trust?"

She scrunched up her nose and said, "You're acting like I'm crazy. Like I'm totally out of my lane here."

"What? No, I never — I never said —"

"What about the girl the summer after high school, Andie? What about the lingering looks, the touches, the phone calls that came at all hours of the day and night?"

I flushed. Erika had been a blight on my marriage. I hadn't slept with her or even kissed her, but she was obsessed with me. She'd followed me around school, misinterpreting every kind gesture or polite thing I said as encouragement. As flirting. Then, when we graduated, she started working at the convenience store near our house. I saw her almost every day when I stopped in for coffee. Somehow, she got my phone number. I never figured out how.

"Nothing happened," I told Joy, and it was the truth.

"She couldn't stop contacting you," Joy replied. "We had to get a restraining order. We had to go to *court*."

I dragged a hand down my face. Not this again. I didn't want to just keep circling the drain, trying to keep this ship afloat. When we first got together, it had been easy. I missed that.

We were different people now. Maybe that was the big problem.

I thought about Liv. I was thinking a lot more about her lately — and not just about her case. When I looked at my wife, with her pale skin and blonde hair, blue eyes, and thin eyebrows, I'm shaken by the stark contrast between her and Liv.

I shouldn't have been thinking about Liv at that moment.

I should have been focused on Joy.

"Where are you?" Joy asked softly. "I want to reach you, but I can't get through."

"I'm sorry," I said, even though I wasn't.

"So am I," she answered, even though she wasn't either.

I blinked back stinging tears. "We can't just keep hurting each other like this. I don't want to be this person, Joy. I don't like who I am, and I don't want to put you through this."

"Me neither," Joy said. "Maybe... maybe it's time we called it off."

My heart thudded painfully. I wasn't sure whether the flutter in my stomach was excitement, or fear, or both.

"So," I said. "We're... doing this?"

We both knew that this conversation had been a long time

coming. We were having more and more stupid fights evolving from our bickering. We'd had some screaming matches. Neither of us had signed up to love the people we'd become.

"We're doing this," Joy said.

I slipped the gold ring off my finger. It came off easily. I dropped it into the trinket dish with a satisfying plink.

I thought I'd feel more at the dissolution of my marriage, but the overwhelming grief and guilt I'd braced for never came. All I felt was a smug sense of triumph. I wasn't sure what that said about the kind of woman I was.

Joy held up her hand. On it, I saw the telltale tan line of wear her ring had once been. God knows how long it had been since she'd worn it.

"Better late than never," she murmured.

I let out a breath I felt like I'd been holding for a decade. It had been such a long time since I'd felt anything but numb about my life. Maybe Joy was right. Maybe things would finally be good from here on out. Now, thinking about Liv didn't feel like a betrayal. It didn't feel terrible. It felt *right*.

Joy's eyes were red, and her face was wet with tears. I sniffled and realized that I was crying too, though for how long, I had no idea. I looked at Joy then and I saw *her*, the girl I'd fallen in love with all those years ago. The girl in the bleachers with the bow in her hair and the smile so bright it was blinding. I saw the girl I'd risked everything for, just for the chance to be legally hers. I saw her and my heart broke. It broke for all we'd been and everything we'd been through. Most of all, it broke for the future we'd never have.

"I don't hate you," Joy said. "I think... I think that if I hated you, this would all be easy. If one of us had done something..." Her voice trailed off. She was crying again — though I could only tell by the way she was breathing.

"Yeah," I said. "It would be much easier."

But we had never built our relationship on *easy*.

Joy flipped the lever to drain the bathtub. She sat still in the bubbles as the water gurgled down the drain. Her face had softened and she looked more relaxed and relieved than I'd seen her in years.

I put the lid down on the toilet and sat, just looking at her for a minute.

"There's no one else?" Joy asked.

I wanted to lie. I wanted to tell the truth. But I didn't know what either of those was, so I gave her all I could.

"Liv Reyes," I said. "I can't get her out of my head. But she..."

"She's a case," Joy finished. "And you're married."

"Yes." I settled my hands on my thighs.

Joy exhaled in a rush. She pulled herself out of the tub and grabbed her towel. Despite having seen her naked hundreds of times, I didn't watch her dry off. Given how our relationship was changing, it felt like a violation, an invasion of her privacy.

Besides, there was also the risk her body would make me lose my nerve. She'd used it against me before. Even if it seemed like we were on the same page now, I didn't want desire to make me go back on my word. It felt like a power imbalance — her standing, me sitting; me clothed, her naked.

Everything worked itself out.

"You bought the house," Joy said. "Do you want... I mean, I could move out."

I shook my head. "Don't be silly. I can bunk with my parents or something."

"Really? You'd put in more time with your dad?"

I looked at her then, and she smirked. I couldn't help smirking, too.

"That's a valid point," I said.

"I'll find somewhere to go," she said. "Don't worry, Andie. You know me. I'm tough. I can handle myself."

She had a point, but it was hard. She'd already had a hard go of it in life, and I hated the thought that I'd be adding more weight to her already heavy burden. After all, her family here wasn't speaking to her. They hadn't even come to our wedding.

"You don't have to worry about all that anymore," Joy added.

"I'll always worry about you." It felt like the most honest thing I'd ever said to her. We stayed there staring at each other, looking into each other's eyes, and both of us started crying again. I got up from the toilet and pulled her into my arms. I couldn't remember the last time I'd hugged her before this. Her arms went around my neck and she leaned against me, pressing her chest against mine.

Warmth flooded my veins. I loved her. But loving meant leaving sometimes.

I let Joy have the bed, but the couch was too lumpy for me to sleep on. Cursing myself for not having spent a little more money on good furniture, I got up and paced for a while. Eventually, I realized I wasn't getting any sleep and changed into my uniform and slipped out of the house, careful not to let the screen door slam behind me. On the way to the station, I didn't even turn on the radio. I didn't call anyone. I drove in silence.

I'd just experienced the most painful breakup of my life, but I was ready to move on. I was ready to tell Liv everything — what she meant to me, what she'd done for me, and how I planned to pay her back. I knew that getting with her meant I couldn't work on the investigation any longer, but I didn't care. I hoped she wouldn't, either. In the grand scheme of things, hadn't we discovered something so much better?

I kept thinking about Liv, about everything she'd said to me — and everything she hadn't. I thought about the sharp planes of her face and the fullness of her lips.

It was two in the morning when I got out of my car and walked into the precinct. Officer Paul Wesson was at the front desk paging through some files. He stood when I entered.

"You're not on call," he said.

"I know," I said. "I broke out of the zoo. You gonna tell on me?"

He laughed. "Like Alameda would believe me. You're a workaholic."

"Don't I know it," I said. "Who do you think I got it from?"

Wesson's forehead creased as he studied me. "Something wrong?" he asked.

I hesitated. Wesson was one of the few people in the precinct who knew what I was going through in my relationship with Joy. He'd gone to school with us. He knew us both, and he'd been there from the beginning. It made sense to let him in.

He didn't know about Liv, though. Only Lyle and my dad did.

"I can't get this case out of my head," I said. "It should have gone to you."

Even as I said it, I knew it wasn't true. There was no way that Wesson or anyone else would have believed what Liv said about the sirens.

But I did. I couldn't help it.

If the sirens hadn't killed the kids, it meant that Liv had, and I refused to believe that she was capable of that. I wasn't stupid. I knew that people could snap. I also knew that there were plenty of killers walking around, going to work, and paying their taxes like everyone else. I'd read about Ted Bundy, Jeffrey Dahmer, Joseph D'Angelo. Liv wasn't like that.

She might have been a lot of things, but she couldn't be a killer.

Wesson sighed and rested a hand on top of the file he'd been reading. "He put me on your petty theft."

"You're joking," I said, eyebrows raised.

"Nope. Chief said we need to move on it, and since you're dealing with the Reyes incident..." He shrugged. "We used to be partners. I guess it makes sense."

Partners. Shit, I still had one of those, and she was even more in the dark about Liv than Wesson. If I wanted to stand a chance of getting someone else to believe in and listen to Liv, I had to get Lyle on my side. I had to let her in, no matter what she thought.

82

I shook my head, refocused on Wesson. "I'm sorry, Paul. Hopefully it won't take much longer."

"We made an arrest yesterday."

"Was it that Hogan guy?"

"Yeah. The accomplice you found rolled over on him."

"My instincts were right," I said. Despite my not being on the case, I felt a rush of pride.

"Looks like it," he said.

"Thanks for letting me know."

Beyond him, I could hear the business of the precinct—the hum of the air conditioner, the clicking of keyboards, the chime of the coffeemaker announcing its job completed. Even at such a weird time of the night, my coworkers put in the hours.

"Is Lyle here?" I asked.

"Haven't seen her around, but I don't know her schedule. Might want to check upstairs."

"Thanks, Wesson."

"Don't mention it."

I started to walk toward the stairs, but then I stopped and I faced Wesson again. "Hey," I said. "Do you know who's working security for the witness in my case?"

Wesson's jaw tightened. "You know I'm not supposed to share that information with just anyone, McCollum."

"Alameda now," I corrected. "And I'm not anyone."

"Okay, *Alameda Now*," said Wesson. "But you're not getting me in trouble."

"You're bad at keeping secrets," I said. "Can't you tell me this one?"

He sighed, lowering his voice even further as he said, "Okay, fine. I'll spill. Tonight, it's supposed to be Lyle."

"Oh," I said. Of course it was. I don't even know what I was thinking. Still, I knew my partner. I knew how to get into her head.

"Why do you ask?" Wesson said.

Oh, no reason. I just want to get some one-on-one time with a person of interest free from prying eyes.

"She trusts me," I said. "Ms. Reyes. More than anyone else."

I could tell Wesson was already having second thoughts, but that meant he planned to tell me what I wanted to know, anyway. I knew he could get in serious trouble for breaching protocol like this, and I didn't take that lightly. I might have had a keen interest in Liv, but I wasn't going to let that fact cost either of us our jobs.

Wesson leaned in close, lowering his voice even more. I had to strain to hear it. "If you want to take over the detail from Lyle, I'd approach her directly."

I nodded. "Thanks, Paul."

"Don't mention it. Really, Andie." His expression darkened. "Leave me out of this one."

I nodded again and ventured farther into the station. After almost a decade working in the same building, I thought I knew exactly where Lyle sat. She was on the ground floor, her desk butting up against the women's restroom. She deserved better, but I digressed.

Dawsonville was a boys' club. That was how it had been for my father, and the issue and the attitudes persisted through the years. If you were a female cop, you didn't get the cushiest digs, the best cruiser, or the best gear. Hell, you were lucky to get a parking space. I'd tried raising concerns about the state of things to my dad before, but he hadn't listened.

"I hire lots of women," he'd said. "And some of the best cops I *know* are women."

I'd tried to tell him that didn't change the facts. It was still dire straits for female cops at the DPD. He hadn't listened, and I stopped bringing it up. I hadn't felt like fighting. Now, I wondered if I'd given up too easily.

Lyle was sitting at her desk, reading something on her monitor.

"Hey," I said.

"Oh, hey," she answered.

"Could I steal you for a second?"

"Sure thing. I was just catching up on emails." She twisted in her chair to face me. Her warm brown eyes glinted. "What's on your mind?"

"Liv Reyes," I said.

"What about her?"

"She's... you're on security detail for her, right?"

Lyle's eyes narrowed. "Yeah," she said, hesitant. "Why?"

"I was wondering if you might want to trade shifts," I said. God, I hoped my voice sounded as nonchalant as possible. "I'm not scheduled right now. I'm supposed to come in at one p.m."

Lyle glanced at the clock, frowning. "Why would you want to do that?" she asked. "You don't like overnights."

"Sure I do," I said. "Let's just say I can't sleep. I'd rather be productive while I'm wide awake."

"I don't know," Lyle said. "Chief—your dad—he said he wanted me on this detail. Like, me specifically."

Somehow, I doubted that. Dad had too many other things on his plate to care much about a standard security detail.

"She's not officially in protected custody," I said.

"No, she isn't," Lyle agreed. "Not officially."

"The witness and I," I started. "We've developed a rapport. She has a hard time trusting people." I lowered my voice. "She wants someone she knows looking out for her. I'm sure you understand that."

"I get it," Lyle said, "but I don't want to be in hot water with your dad."

"You won't be, all right? He won't even know. You think he checks the schedules?" Hell, I knew he didn't. When I'd still been living at home, I hadn't seen him so much as glance at the officers' schedules.

"He wanted me on this shift," Lyle repeated. Shit, I was losing her. I had to act fast.

"I'll take your evidence locker inventory duty for a month," I said.

"Damn," said Lyle. "You really want this."

"So, what do you say?" I asked.

After another moment of consideration, Lyle sighed. "If I don't sign this over to you now, I feel like you'll get what you want anyway," she said. "I might as well cooperate and get out of inventory."

I grinned at her. "And you get to go home and sleep. The icing on the cake."

"You're welcome," she said. "Just don't tell the chief."

The Sunset Inn was not on the safest or the cleanest side of town. It was only forty-five bucks a night, which was why the DPD usually put witnesses up there. By the time I pulled into the deserted parking lot, early dawn's pink fingers stretched across the sky. I had no idea what I was doing there. All I knew was that I wanted to see Liv, and I wanted to do that without outside intervention. I meant everything I'd said about her trusting me.

I also knew that if Dad found out what I was doing—especially after I'd insisted I wasn't in over my head—he'd boot my ass from the station.

Liv was worth the risk.

I hesitated after I unclipped my seatbelt. My cell phone glowed on the console. I had Liv's number; I'd snagged it from her contact sheet. Maybe I should call her or shoot her a text, if only to let her know I was here. If she was sleeping or if she decided she didn't want to see me after all, it would save me the devastation of hearing it in person.

After all our conversations, I didn't think she could deny the tension between us. Even though we hadn't acknowledged it outright, all signs seem to point toward her feeling like I did. To her wanting more from me. So, I'd come here. God only knew what would happen next, but at least I'd gotten the ball rolling. I picked up my phone and dialed the number before I could stop myself.

Liv answered on the third ring, her voice rough and thick with sleep.

"Hello?" she said.

"Liv," I said. "It's me. It's Sergeant—it's Andie."

"Andie," Liv said. "Jesus. Is something going on?"

I realized then that I had no real pretext for getting her number. She hadn't given it to me. I'd stolen it from work. Of course she'd think I was calling her with news about the case.

I swallowed. "Everything's fine. Did I wake you up?"

"No," she said. I couldn't tell if she was lying. "Why are you calling? Did something happen?"

"Can I come in?" I asked.

I had no idea which room she was in; that wasn't in the file. As I spoke, I peered up at the curtained motel windows, straining to see movement, or her face peeking out.

"You're here?" she asked.

"The Sunset Inn," I said, reading the sign. "Dawsonville's finest."

Liv chuckled at that. "Hang on, I'll let you in. Room 206."

I was a little surprised by how well this was going. I still hadn't told her the real reason I was there. Then again, I wasn't even sure I knew the reason anymore. Liv hung up, and so did I. Right before I could set my cellphone down again, it vibrated loudly. I checked the screen: Joy.

My pulse quickened. I wasn't sure I was ready to talk to her again. After all, I'd left the house in the middle of the night. I hadn't even decided if I was going to go back.

I also felt a twinge of guilt. I'd mentioned Liv to Joy, and it felt like I'd tainted whatever Liv and I were building. I didn't want to destroy it like I had my marriage.

Before I realized what I was doing, I hit the green phone button and held the phone to my ear again. "Yeah?"

"God, I... I was worried about you," Joy said. "I woke up to get a drink of water and you weren't on the couch. Scared the shit out of me."

"I'm okay," I said. "I just couldn't sleep."

"Did you go into work?" she asked.

"Yeah." I scratched the side of my face. "I didn't know what else to do."

"I thought you were seeing her," said Joy.

"I am seeing her," I admitted. There was a long pause. Maybe she'd hung up, or the call had disconnected. "Joy?"

"It feels empty without you here," she said. "We used to be so happy. When did we stop?"

I didn't know what to say. I didn't know when we'd changed, but we had. Maybe I was the only one who had changed. But there was no going back.

"I don't know, Joy," I said.

"Are you coming home later?" she asked.

"I don't know," I said again. There was a long pause. We said our goodbyes and hung up. I felt like my guts had been wrung out like a washcloth. Bile burned the back of my throat.

How had this happened to us? One minute it was the two of us against the world, two small-town lesbians holding hands at football games, attending prom together, and kissing at our lockers. The next thing I knew, we were rocketing toward divorce, and it was my fault.

It was *her* fault, too. But that wasn't how it felt.

Phone hand, I debated texting Liv to say I wasn't coming after all, but I couldn't do it. Instead, I slipped the cell phone into my pocket, got out of the car, and shut the door.

I wound my way up the stairs to the motel's second floor. Room 206 was at the very end of the hall, right next to the elevator and the ice machine. The curtains were drawn, and the placard hanging from her door handle said DO NOT DISTURB. I hesitated.

Shit. Was it too late to turn back?

Get it together, Andie.

I raised my fist to knock, but the door swung inward. Liv stood on the other side in a baggy T-shirt that hung to her mid-thighs. Her hair was mussed from sleep, and her eyelids looked heavy. Seeing her spurred me onward.

"Andie," she said. I loved the way my name sounded coming from her. "Please, come in. I just woke up. Sorry the room is a mess."

Once I'd entered and the door closed, I took a moment to get the lay of the land. It wasn't messy, despite Liv's apology. The motel room was standard with two double beds, generic artwork, and a bathroom with a fluorescent light that flickered every so often. A tiny television was perched on a dresser in front of one of the beds. On the floor was a suitcase overflowing with clothes. It looked as though it had exploded. One of the beds was unmade, the heinous comforter stripped off and lying on the floor. The sheets were rumpled, and the pillow still held the indentation from her head.

Damn, I *had* woken her up.

"To what do I owe the pleasure?" Liv drawled. She stood with her hands on her hips, but she was smiling. I'd never seen her this relaxed.

"I was in the neighborhood," I lied, then remembered that I was going for honesty. I bit my lip and tried again. "I wanted to see you. I don't... I wish I had a better reason, but I can't get you out of my head. I wanted to see how you were doing."

"Isn't that what you do at the station?" she asked.

My pulse quickened. I didn't want to just come out and say it, but maybe I didn't have any other choice. The lump in my throat and the tightness in my chest made it hard to breathe. If I didn't get the words out now, who knew what would happen?

"I didn't want to do it at the station," I said.

Liv's eyes widened, then she frowned. "Are you here to escort me there?"

"Yes," I answered. "Wait, I mean-—no." I paused. "I mean, yes, I'll take you to the station if you want, but that isn't why."

She regarded me carefully, letting her arms fall by her sides. "Is this about my statement?"

"No."

"And it's off the record?" she asked.

"Yes." I paused. "Nothing either of us says or does will get back to the chief, or anyone at the station. I'm not here as a cop right now."

Her eyes were so dark and so deep they could drown me. Liv took a step closer, and I held my breath. "Andie," she said. "What's on your mind?"

Now or never, I thought.

"You," I said.

I looked into her eyes and the whole world tilted. I had to keep talking or I'd never get this out, and then it would just keep festering between the two of us. It was making me a shitty cop and I didn't want to be so shitty anymore.

"I can't— I can't stop thinking about you, Liv. About your hair, your eyes. Your eyebrows. How your face scrunches up when you cry, and how it breaks my heart each time." I let my gaze drop. Her legs were trembling slightly. "I'm always looking for excuses to spend more time with you, and the closer we get to wrapping up your case, the more afraid I am about this... thing between us ending."

Even after I finished taking Liv's statement, she'd stay a witness on the case. Her involvement would continue. So, why was I so anxious?

"Look at me," Liv said. I raised my gaze to meet hers. Her skin was flushed. I wanted to touch her cheek, to feel how hot it was, but I held myself back.

"When the case is over," she said. "I don't want us to be, too."

Us. I could've flown.

My heart pounded like a hammer striking it home. "Is that okay?" I asked.

"Yeah," she said, letting out a shaky laugh. Her voice was tight, and her eyes shone with unshed tears. "Yeah, Andie. It's more than okay. I can't stop thinking about you, either."

I grinned at her and asked, "You mean it?"

"Come on. You know me well enough by now. I don't say what I don't mean."

She had a point. Still, I could hardly believe it. I'd never felt this way for anyone besides my wife, and even then, it had been ages ago. It was a terrifying onslaught of feelings to face. The only consolation was that Liv felt it, too.

She'd said it was *more than okay*. She felt the same way about me.

"But... you *are* married," she added.

"I broke things off with my wife," I said. "I did it all for you. It's over."

"I never asked you to do that," Liv said. "I never would've—"

"I know."

She grabbed my face and kissed me.

From: **Paul Wesson** <pwesson@dpd.gov>
To: **Roger Alameda** <ralameda@dpd.gov>,
Clarissa Lyle <clyle@dpd.gov>
Subject: **Concerns**

Thu, November 17, 2022, 6:45 am

Chief Alameda and Officer Lyle,

I'm writing to you before my nerves get the
better of me.

I just had a strange interaction with
Sergeant McCollum, and I thought the two of
you needed to know.

Clarissa, I know you'd complained about the
sergeant's involvement with the Reyes incident. Chief, off the record, Officer Lyle and
I had several discussions about the case and
Sergeant Alameda's interviews. It wasn't
until today that I realized how valid her
concerns were.

Sergeant McCollum has gone to the Sunset Inn,
where Ms. Reyes has been staying, alone. She
said nothing about her intentions at the
motel.

I humbly request that you replace me as
Lyle's partner. Sergeant McCollum is too
close to this now, and I have no conflicts of
interest. I've worked with Sergeant McCollum
and should be able to make sense of her notes
in the file. I'm willing to consult with

Officer Lyle if she deems it appropriate as well.

If we don't do something about Sergeant McCollum, Liv Reyes might get away with murder.

Sincerely,

Sergeant Wesson

ANDIE

For the duration of the ride back to the precinct, all I could think about was the softness and warmth of Liv's lips and how good they felt pressed against mine. When Liv and I got back to the station, Wesson was nowhere to be found. I was glad about that. I worried he'd ask why I'd insisted on seeing Liv by myself. I didn't want to lie to him, but I would.

Since meeting Liv, my morals had become a lot more flexible. It should've bothered me, but it didn't.

Thankfully, I didn't see Dad when we entered, either. Unfortunately, I did see my partner standing at my desk, rifling through a file folder. "Officer Lyle," I greeted. Liv's hand brushed mine. I wrangled the urge to grab it.

"Hey," Lyle said, looking at Liv instead of me. "What are you —Alameda, are you working detail?"

Alameda. That meant Wesson had spoken to her. I hesitated. I really didn't want to lie.

"Temporarily," I said. It was the best I could do. "Liv—Miss Reyes—requested me as her escort."

"Oh," Lyle said. "All right. Are you ready for another interview with her?"

I glanced at Liv. She wasn't smiling anymore. I knew she

wasn't eager to get back into talking about the worst part of her life.

"You should probably ask her," I said. "Not me."

Meekly, Liv nodded. I felt bad for her. We kept reopening a wound she needed sewn shut.

Lyle didn't come with us. I figured she had something else to do. It didn't matter to me.

"We can take our time," I said, leading Liv to the interview room that had begun to feel like my second home. The time I'd spent interviewing Liv was the most time I'd spent in an interview room in seven years of policing. I wasn't eager to cause her any more pain, but I knew we had to get the rest of the story out there. I had to know what happened next, or else I couldn't save her.

"Where were we?" Liv asked as if she'd been telling me some wild joke and not the painful story of how all her friends had died.

I lowered my voice. "Liv, if you need more time... I mean, if you don't want to do this now—or if you don't want to do this with me—"

"No." Liv waved me off. "This isn't about you. It's not about us. It..." Her voice trailed off. I waited for her to say more, but she didn't.

"Claire," I prompted. "We left off with Claire."

LIV

I staggered through the opening and somehow squeezed past the plane wing. I hadn't stopped swimming since Sidney let me go, and I kept on swimming until I reached the shores of the safe spot. Alex was there. He wasn't asleep anymore. Instead, he'd found something to read.

"A-Alex," I stammered. "I— Claire is... we—"

"Later," he cut me off. I was surprised by that. Alex never interrupted me, especially when he knew I had something pretty significant to say. Still, I was glad for the interruption. God only knew how I was going to tell him about what had happened, how we'd almost sacrificed him, and how Claire had still died for the plan, only for it all to fail.

I didn't know how to tell him that he and I were the only survivors.

For now, nagged a voice at the back of my mind. I tried not to listen.. If I gave up in the bunker, the sirens would kill me, and there'd be no closure for my friends' families, or for mine. If I gave up, there would be no one to stop this from happening to someone else.

"What did you find?" I asked.

He didn't answer. Instead, he waved me over to him. I came,

leaning over his shoulder and trying to read the book he held. It was a three-ring binder filled with warped and wrinkled paper. It didn't look like the kind of thing that should've been thrown away; it must've been taken from or abandoned by someone who'd once frequented the bunker.

"It's a lab report," Alex said. "A bunch of them. Dated kind of long ago. They're all about the sirens, Liv. They knew about the sirens."

My heart beat so hard I imagined it cracking my sternum.

"Why didn't anyone else, then?" I asked.

I couldn't fathom how someone in the scientific community might have discovered what we'd found and kept quiet about it.

I checked the date over Alex's shoulder. The last journal entry went back to 1956. Surely we would've heard a conspiracy theory or something.

I remembered the pile of bones. I couldn't stop thinking about them.

"Fuck," I said. "The sirens must've eaten them."

"Maybe," Alex said. He was either deluded or kidding himself. Sure, he hadn't seen the bones, but he'd seen everything else they'd done. He knew the story couldn't possibly have a happy ending.

"I don't think they just walked out of here," I said. Alex flipped through the journal, eyes dragging over each page. I followed along as he studied the words on the paper.

"I'll read some of this," he said. "I think you should hear it."

"Okay," I agreed. " I'll settle in then."

I sat beside him on the sand and listened to him read.

"The sirens didn't always live in the bunker," Alex said. I'd figured as much, but the writing confirmed it.

"What else does it say?" I asked.

He skimmed the pages, turning them as he spoke. "They... they wanted to weaponize the sirens."

"What?" I asked. It was hard to believe.

Alex cleared his throat and read from the journal directly.

"'We remain optimistic that these trials won't be in vain. Eisenhower said we're the best men for this, and I don't want to let him down. We'll keep exposing the creatures to radiation until we get what we want.'"

"What's that supposed to mean?" I asked.

Alex shrugged. "The last entry here... it should tell us what happened to them." He continued: "'One of the creatures broke free of its tank. Johannson is dead. Porter is gravely injured. I heard more glass shatter an hour ago, people screaming, equipment crashing to the floor—but I'm not man enough to face it. I'm hiding in a closet. If this is how I die, tell my Carol that I love her. Anthony Edward Black.'"

Once Alex closed the journal, the two of us just sat there. It was clear that the sirens had escaped their containment—had gotten revenge on the scientists who trapped them there—but knowing that didn't change much.

I don't know how long we sat there. Without the sun or any natural light, it was hard to tell what time it was. We both had our phones, but the water had destroyed them; mine wouldn't even turn on anymore. Alex's phone might have displayed the time, but the screen was shattered, and we couldn't read a thing on it.

Somehow, I felt less pessimistic than I had before the journal. Maybe I shouldn't have, but I felt smarter than the scientists. Superior somehow. Because we had *survived*.

"I have an idea," I said.

Alex lifted his head. "You have a plan, you mean?"

"Well, I'm working on it," I said. "I need your help."

"Let me check my calendar," he joked.

"Pencil me in," I answered, tracing figures in the sand with the tip of my finger. Our hands were close enough to touch. I wanted to take Alex's hand in mine, but it didn't feel right. Maybe when we got out, I could tell him the truth. I'd let him know how I felt about him. Maybe then, he'd feel the same about me.

Confessing my feelings didn't seem so scary anymore.

"It's do or die now, isn't it?" Alex asked.

I pressed my lips together. "Might be do *and* die if we can't figure this out."

"What do you think we should do?" Alex asked. I wasn't quite sure how to answer.

All I could think about was what had happened earlier with Claire; how the sirens had tricked us.

We could do it. We could trick them. Or we could trick one of them, at least. If we got one, we'd get them all, and then we might get out of there.

I stretched my legs out in front of me. My shins burned, and a dull ache spread through my kneecaps. "What if we could trick the sirens?"

Alex raised an eyebrow. "What do you mean?"

"Hear me out," I said. "Earlier, Claire and I— we convinced Harper to let us out. We got through to her—or, we thought we did, anyway."

"How did you manage that?" Alex asked. I pressed my lips together, tried not to remember the plaintive edge to Claire's voice as they tore her apart, and failed.

"We... well, we told Harper if she let us go, we'd bring more people to them."

"*Bring them* as in *sacrifice them*."

"Obviously, yes." I scratched the side of my face. "It seemed like it worked. I mean, Harper ultimately tricked us, but if we'd tried the approach on someone just a little more naïve..." I let my voice trail off. Alex's brow furrowed.

"You think we could pull it off this time," he said.

"I think it's worth a shot," I said. "We might not be able to go all the way with it, but at least we'd have an edge to murder one of them or something."

I couldn't believe what I was saying, except that I could. After everything we'd been through—after every awful thing that they'd done to my friends—I was eager to make a bitch bleed.

Alex considered the plan for a moment. The only sounds I

heard were the lapping waves against the shore and the pounding of my heartbeat in my ears.

"We should try it on Sidney," Alex said. "She's most likely to believe us."

I nodded. "The other two— they're also more likely to protect her. If we even threaten her, I think the others will come running." I paused. "That also means that once we start this thing, we have to be ready."

"It's better than dying of thirst," he said. At that point, I wasn't so sure. Saying so wouldn't help us, though. And he had a point; I'd rather go down fighting. If they were going to eat us, I wanted to make them work for it.

"What can we use?" I asked, craning my neck to look at the debris along the wall. Besides the journal, all we had was some mangled, waterlogged office furniture—not exactly the armory I would've killed for, pun intended.

"Not as much as I'd like," he answered. "Maybe we can make a weapon out of the rusted metal. Have you had your tetanus shot?"

I laughed. "And hepatitis."

"At least we're safe from those, then," said Alex, one side of his mouth lifted in a smile. At that moment, I saw the shadow of the Alex from before, the one I'd known since we were children. The one I'd loved for years. As I looked at him, my stomach twisted.

This plan was do or die. We had to be ready. There was no going back.

I thought again about making my peace with everything, maybe telling Alex how I felt about him.

It would have to wait. For now, we had a plan to put together.

Alex got up and brushed the sand off his pants. He walked back toward the pile of debris with his arms crossed over his chest, considering. I watched him for a moment before getting up, shaking the sand from my clothes, and joining him.

He was right—we didn't seem to have that much to work

with. I wasn't sure how much we could cobble together from so few resources.

I took a look around. We were in a cave. Water dripped from the ceiling, sliding down moss-covered walls. I glanced over at the plane. At the crack in the wall.

"Shit," Alex hissed.

"Tell me about it."

The chill in the air made me shiver, and as I searched the ceiling for another way out, I realized we didn't have one.

This idea with Sidney was our only option. It seemed ludicrous, especially with how sleep-deprived I felt. Still, we couldn't afford to be picky.

Alex was eyeing the pile of debris like it was the most confusing thing he'd ever seen.

"Any ideas?" I asked.

"Hang on," he said. "I'll get back to you."

He went to the pile and ran his hands over the smooth surface of the desk, frowning. His eyes skimmed the garbage that surrounded it before landing on the metal folding chair. It was rusted beyond belief, the metal weak from years of water and radiation and God only knew what else. Alex stuck his foot on the metal crossbar at the side of the legs. He grabbed the top of the chair with both hands and pushed down, snapping the metal. A sharp bar stuck out from one of the legs. He looked up at me and nodded.

"Found our weapon," he said.

"Is it sharp enough?" I asked. The closer we got to acting on our plan, the more hesitant I became. What if it didn't work? We had no clue what we were doing. Besides that, could I stab someone? The sirens were monsters, but they were thinking, breathing beings.

My resolve wavered. Alex must have seen it on my face because he let go of the chair and headed back toward me.

"Liv," he said, taking me by the shoulders. "Hey, we'll get through this."

I nodded. "We have to."

"I'll take care of you," he said.

"And I'll take care of you."

He smiled with more confidence than I felt and headed back up to the chair. His footsteps left tracks in the sand, and I stared at them.

Alex held the bar out for my inspection. Rust had eaten most of it, but the end looked solid. It was sharp, too, but not nearly enough. I didn't know anything about the sirens' skin, but I wasn't sure that the metal could pierce it.

"We should sharpen it somehow," I said.

"I don't think we can," he said.

We both looked around. It wasn't like someone had dropped a giant knife sharpener down in the bunker. I couldn't even see a stone to use, not that I even knew what I was looking for.

"The wall," Alex said. He reached out, sliding his hand over it. "It's concrete, but it's tougher here. We might be able to make it work."

I chewed the inside of my cheek. Pain flared up through my shins. The last thing I needed was a flare.

Alex scraped the end of the bar against the wall until it sharpened into a point. Once he'd finished, he studied his handiwork before holding it out to me.

I nodded. "Looks good."

"No time like the present," Alex said. "Let's slip out and try it."

"Leave the talking to me, for the most part," I said. "I'll go with what worked last time."

"Fine by me," Alex agreed. "Let's do it."

Alex tucked the rod into the back of his pants. We walked down to the shoreline together. With one look at each other before we stepped into the water again, I took the opportunity to grab his hand. He threaded our fingers together like we'd done this a thousand times.

"Ready?" he asked.

"I have to be," I answered.

Something shifted in his expression—a flicker of softness in his eyes—but then the steel edge of determination replaced it. Without another word, the two of us waded into the water.

As I kicked and propelled us toward the hole in the wall, I realized the chill of the water cut into my legs like a razor. My nerves cursed me with each movement, and a muscle spasm started in my right thigh.

"Fuck," I said.

"You okay?" he asked.

"Yeah," I said. "It's just my fibro."

He squeezed my hand. "Should I do this alone?"

Embarrassment would've made me blush if the water hadn't been so cold. Jesus, it was freezing. Without adrenaline as insulation, it was hardly bearable.

"Never," I told him. "I'll be all right."

Together, we moved the plane wing aside and slipped out into the deeper water. My heart leaped into my throat, making it hard to breathe. It was so deep here that we had to tread water, which I couldn't do for long; my muscles would give up.

"There might be a handhold there." Alex gestured toward the wall. "Maybe we should check it out."

I didn't want to let go of his hand. I didn't want him to have to face this mess alone, even for a moment. We were all each other had now. He must have seen or sensed my reluctance then because he sighed.

"I'll head over there with you,'" he said. "We need to keep talking to attract attention, though. If they didn't hear us moving the plane, we won't be able to draw them out."

But that wasn't the only way. It was just the safest option, and safe options had gotten us nowhere, and I was tired of being trapped.

Before Alex could stop me, I thrust the palm of my hand into the sharp end of the pole. It punctured my skin with a bite, shooting off alarm bells in my brain. It hurt a lot more than I'd expected it to, and I was glad I'd thought quickly enough not to use my wrist. If I had, that might've killed me.

Alex and I made eye contact.

"What the hell are you doing?" he asked.

I winced, grabbing the pole with my free hand while I slowly dragged it out of the wound it had made. Blood pooled in my palm and spilled into the water, blooming in rusty red tendrils around me. "They can smell our blood," I said.

Together, we waited.

Drawn in by the blood, a siren swam toward us. I spotted the fin right away, though I couldn't tell who it belonged to. Even after all we'd seen, a shiver of revulsion traveled down my spine.

All I kept thinking was that if this didn't work—if Alex couldn't get the timing right, or if the makeshift spear didn't do its job—this siren could still tear me apart.

There was also the chance that, even if Alex did get the timing right, and this siren died right away, her sisters could still rip both of us apart. It occurred to me then that we should have thought this out a little more, that we should have had a backup plan.

"Fuck," Alex said like he knew exactly what I was thinking.

"You think this is a bad idea?" I asked.

"We don't have a better one," said Alex.

I hesitated. "Listen, Alex. If this... if this doesn't work, there's something I want you to know."

"Tell me later," he said.

"But what if—"

"You heard me."

The siren could've easily dragged me to the bottom by herself, tearing me into pieces with Alex none the wiser, but I'd counted on her not being able to stop herself from toying with us first. So far, my bet was paying off.

At last, Sidney's head popped up, water slicking her hair back from her face. Her eyes were full black, the pupils swallowing the irises whole.

"Hello, little fishes," she said. "Knew you'd come out sometime."

"We didn't have a choice," Alex said. "Liv's hurt. We want out. We have a proposition for you."

Sidney licked her lips. "You don't have long. I'm not that patient."

"Let us go," I said, "and... and we'll bring you more people to eat."

I was also realizing that this plan depended on the sirens keeping secrets from each other, which was nowhere near a safe assumption for us to make. If Harper had told them anything about what happened with me and Claire earlier, there was no way that this plan would work.

Shit.

Alex's hip pressed against mine in the water. He kept me focused on the present.

"Think about it," I continued. "You can eat us, but what if no one else comes down here? There can't be too much else around to eat. We'd... we'd make it worth your while."

"We could even work out some kind of schedule," Alex said. "Bring somebody down every couple of days, maybe. That way, you'll never run out of food."

Something flashed in Sidney's eyes. "You'd sacrifice others to us?"

"We don't love the idea," I said. "But it makes the most sense."

I looked back at Alex, silently pleading for him to get ready. Sidney was almost close enough to touch now, and just about as close as I wanted her to get to us before he stabbed her.

"Shake on it," Sidney said. She stretched a hand toward us. I took it, pulling her toward me in one smooth movement. Out of the corner of my eye, I saw Alex raise the metal bar. A shadow of fear crossed Sidney's features right before he brought the tip of it into her chest.

Blood exploded like a crimson supernova, coloring the water all around us.

Sidney howled, jerking away from me and thrashing. She clawed at the spear stuck in her chest. It looked like it had gone in between her ribs. Alex's aim had been even better than I'd expected.

Sidney coughed—a wet, hacking sound—and blood trickled from her mouth.

"You got her lung," I said. "Holy shit, Alex. You got her fucking lung."

"If she even has those," he said.

"I don't think it matters."

Sidney coughed again, the sound tapering into a keening wail that reverberated off the bunker's walls and rattled each bone in my body.

"Molly," Sidney wheezed. "And Harper."

"We know," I answered. "We're counting on it."

"Hurry," Alex said.

We swam away from Sidney as fast as we could, not stopping to look back or second-guess ourselves. If we couldn't get to another part of the bunker before the others showed up, we wouldn't stand a chance.

"Alex," I said, voice breaking.

He shushed me. I recognized a corridor that led back where we'd come. It wasn't ideal, but it would do. We had to put more distance between us and the sirens.

Harper called Sidney's name. Alex and I kept swimming.

Another piercing wail broke the bunker's stillness. I exchanged a look with Alex. It wasn't safe to speak for fear of being overheard, but he must have known as well as I did what it meant: They'd found her.

"We don't have much time," Alex whispered. I already knew that. He knew I did. I think it was just his way of trying to take control of a situation that was so far beyond anything either of us was prepared for.

We had to stay focused. We were almost free.

Thinking quickly, I led Alex toward the part of the bunker where Harper had brought Claire and me. Her body—or whatever was left of it—must have still been around somewhere. I hoped to God it wasn't on the platform.

But it was.

I froze in the water, ice flooding my already chilled veins. Harper—or one of her sisters— had heaved Claire's corpse onto the platform. Her body lay face down, one arm hanging off the edge into the water. I wasn't even thankful that we couldn't see her face because the rest of her was awful. Huge, gaping tears and red chasms stretched across her skin. Her ribs stuck out, exposed, some stubborn muscle and tendons clinging to the bone. As we got closer, I saw the puddle of blood around her and noticed—

"Alex," I breathed.

He touched my shoulder. "Is that... is that Claire?"

"It was," I said. "But... it looks like she's breathing."

Claire turned her head. Her eyes were open, and they weren't glazed over. They darted around in their sockets, seeking the source of the splashing noises we made as we approached the platform. Although her ribs stuck out, I saw her back rise and fall. When we were close enough to hear the rasp and rattle of her breaths, Alex grabbed the edge of the platform. His other hand closed on my arm.

"She's still alive," he said.

I couldn't even nod. I was far too stunned. What were we supposed to do? We couldn't leave her there, but she also wasn't in any condition to climb out of the bunker with us. I could only imagine what other injuries she'd sustained. There had to be damage that we couldn't even see.

I exchanged a look with Alex. His eyes were wide and wild.

"What do you think we should do?" I asked. I had a pretty good idea, but it was a dark one, and I didn't want to entertain it if we had another option. At that moment, I was counting on Alex's levelheadedness to get us out of this one, to stop us from killing anybody else.

His Adam's apple bobbed as he swallowed.

"She must be in a lot of pain," he said. Then, to Claire: "Hey, Claire. It's Alex. Can you... can you hear me? Blink twice if you understand."

Claire groaned. She didn't blink, though.

"Fuck," I said.

"She's gone," he said. "The lights are on, but no one's home."

I gripped the edge of the platform. Alex was still holding onto my arm. I didn't want him to let go.

"What should we do?" I asked again, as though, somehow, the answer would change.

"We can't take her with us," Alex said.

"I know," I said. "We could get help and send them back for her, right?"

"Assuming she'd make it that long," said Alex, brow furrowed. "If I'm honest, I don't think she will."

It felt awful talking about Claire like she wasn't right there in front of us, but as Alex had discovered, she couldn't understand what we were saying. Alex was right. She was gone already. There was nothing we could do for her.

Well, there was one thing.

I wished we still had the metal bar, but it was still lodged in Sidney's chest. We'd have to improvise.

With more strength than I thought I had, I pulled myself onto the platform. Water dripped from me as I got on my hands and knees and crawled toward Claire. My heart had plunged into my stomach.

"How are you going to do it?" Alex asked. I wished he hadn't. I hadn't decided yet, and his question only made it feel more real. My stomach turned. I would've vomited if anything had been in it.

"I... I could snap her neck," I said. "I don't know how much

109

force it takes, but I think it would be the quickest. We don't have anything else. I have to use my hands."

"Wait," Alex said. He pulled himself up on the platform, getting on all fours beside me. The sounds of distant splashing echoed off the bunker walls. We were running out of time. "You shouldn't have to do this," Alex said. "Let me take care of it."

"You don't have to," I said.

"Liv, you barely knew her," Alex said "If one of us has to, it should be me." He winced. "Besides, I'm... I'm stronger. I'll make sure it's fast."

Hot tears bubbled over my lashes and streamed down my cheeks. None of this was fair. We were supposed to come down here and shoot some spooky footage. This was supposed to have been a reunion. Instead, it was a nightmare.

Alex's eyes shone with unshed tears. As much as I appreciated him taking the lead, I didn't want him to suffer.

"It's not fair," I said, because it wasn't.

"I know," he said. I think he thought I meant everything else. I guess I did.

Alex knelt beside Claire. She wheezed with each breath, a wet, breathy sound that hurt to hear. I looked at her, and then I looked at Alex. His face was a stoic mask.

"You don't have to do this," I repeated.

"Yeah, I do," he answered. Alex gingerly lifted Claire's head and cradled it in his hands. His arms trembled. My stomach clenched.

Was it better to watch, to get the closure, or should I look away to give them privacy? I had no idea how someone was supposed to behave in this situation. Maybe there wasn't a right way. Maybe I just had to live through it.

Claire's eyes caught the light. I gazed at her, holding her in my sight. If I'd been less of a coward, I might have held her in my arms.

"Shh," Alex said, stroking her hair. "It's all right, Claire. It won't hurt anymore."

Unspoken words pricked the back of my tongue.

I'm sorry we couldn't save you, I thought. *I'm sorry we weren't good enough.*

Alex gasped, and I realized he was fighting back a sob. Tears flowed freely down his face, though his expression hadn't changed. My heart ached for him.

Before another awful moment passed, Alex twisted Claire's head hard until her neck snapped.

I cried out at the sound, burying my face in the crook of my elbow.

Neither of us said anything for a minute. I couldn't lift my head to look at him, and he didn't try to make me.

Alex sniffed and asked, "What now?" His voice was flat, thin, and defeated.

A hellish shriek echoed from where we'd come. It was wholly inhuman, high and little metallic.

"They're coming," I said. "We'd better get ready."

"Do you know where we're going?" Alex asked.

I thought back to Harper's behavior earlier. When she'd led us here, it must have been close enough to the real exit to feel believable. We just had to figure out where the real one was before the sirens found us.

"No," I said. "I mean, I don't know exactly where we're going, but I have a good idea."

"That's better than nothing," Alex said, rubbing the back of his neck. His skin was ashen, and he looked emotionally shot. If we got out of here alive, we'd both need extensive therapy.

I wished we had more time. Claire probably wished that, too.

I raked my eyes across the far side of the bunker wall, searching for a crack or a seam—anything indicating a break in the concrete. If we couldn't find a way out or if we couldn't make one, we were screwed.

A series of loud splashes drifted down the corridor. They were coming. I wasn't sure how they hadn't gotten to us yet, but that didn't mean they wouldn't.

"Nothing?" Alex asked.

"I'm looking," I said.

My gaze darted toward a lighter spot in the bunker's corner. It was too far away for me to tell for sure, but it looked like a patch of light. Maybe a trapdoor or something.

"I need to get over there somehow," I said.

Alex shook his head. "I don't think you should leave the platform. They'll eat us alive."

"I don't think we have a choice."

We'd all but run out of options already. If we didn't get out, we'd never know if it was possible. And so far, this plan seemed like the most promising one to get us out of there.

Or one of us, at least.

If I got out, I wasn't sure how I'd come back for Alex, or how I'd help him up and out of the bunker myself. Still, I guessed that was the least of our problems.

"You bitch!" The epithet bounced off the walls, cocooning us in its rage. Harper's head popped out of the water, her face a mask of hatred. "You killed my fucking sister."

"Where's the other one?" I asked.

"What?" Harper growled. "One wasn't enough for you?"

"You killed my friends," I countered.

"And I loved every second," Harper said. "I'd do it all over again if I could, and when I kill the two of you, I'll drag it out. I want you to suffer."

Molly's head popped up beside her sister's. She looked more numb than angry, which surprised me. I'd always thought she was the less rational one, but I guess everyone handled grief in their own way.

"You'll never make it back to the ocean," Alex said.

I recalled what we'd read in the journal, the cruelty the scientists had inflicted on these creatures, and how the sirens responded in kind. Had it been justified? Human scientists had snatched them from their homes and experimented on them without their consent, against their will. They only had each other to rely on in the bunker, and we'd thinned the herd.

If I had to guess, all they wanted was a chance to go back to the ocean. Out there, they'd have all the fish and fauna they could want—a veritable all-you-can-eat buffet. I assumed they wouldn't eat humans if they had access to other food sources, but maybe I was wrong.

It didn't matter.

All that mattered was the broken look that ruined Harper's features.

Her eyes were shining. Tears, I realized in a moment.

"You don't know what we've been through," Harper said.

"You can't imagine it," Molly added.

"I hope you fucking choke on us," I said.

I didn't want to admit it, but I felt like we'd never get out of the bunker. The more time we spent with the sirens, the less sure I was that any plan we tried would work. We'd only been able to overpower Sidney and kill her because she was naïve. We'd also counted on the other sirens being too morose to act, but they both just looked pissed. That didn't bode well for the two of us. But even if we didn't make it out of here alive, the least I could do was hope our bodies killed them.

"I almost don't even want to eat you," Harper said. "I just want to tear you to pieces. Slowly. Let you suffer like you've made us suffer."

"We're killing all of you," said Alex, doubling down. I didn't know where his courage had come from, but I appreciated it. Even if he was just putting on a show for the sirens, it made me feel a little stronger.

I felt Alex's hand brush mine. I laced our fingers together.

If we got nothing else, at least we had that moment.

Harper gripped the edge of the platform, raised herself up, and lunged toward us. Reflexively, Alex and I scrambled backward.

Before I knew what was happening, Alex was torn out of my

grasp and into the water behind us. Sidney and Molly held his arms. He screamed at the same time I did, and we exchanged a look that told me everything I needed to know about Alex Dang: he was going to make sure I made it out of there alive, no matter what it took. Even if it meant he couldn't come with me.

He was more than willing to sacrifice himself for me. I wasn't willing to let him.

Harper looked at me as she swam over to him. I didn't meet her gaze.

Instead, I maintained eye contact with Alex even as Harper latched onto his thigh and ripped out a chunk of meat. The wound was so deep I couldn't help looking. As soon as I did, I saw bone. I was too shocked to vomit.

I stretched and tried to grab his hand, but Harper and Molly were pulling him under. I couldn't look at the blood spraying from his leg; it made me dizzy. You couldn't come back from a wound like that.

My heart wrung itself out. My intestines choked my stomach.

"No," I said.

"H-hey," Alex managed.

Molly pulled him under the water, and I screamed again, clambering to the edge of the platform. Harper's arm shot out. She tried to grab me, too, but I escaped.

I lunged forward again with all my strength, and my stomach slammed against the platform. My chin struck the cement and my teeth clacked together. The metallic tang of blood flowed over my tongue. I turned my head and spit a tooth out. I didn't care about it.

All I cared about was Alex.

Harper tried to grab me again, but instead, I grabbed Alex. I'm still not sure how, but I hauled him up out of the water before they could hurt him more. The water did a lot of the lifting for me.

Alex had scratches on his face and arms from the sirens' claws. The gash in his thigh bubbled wet and red. He was losing a lot of blood and I feared they'd gotten his femoral artery, which meant he had little time.

I pulled him up onto the platform, landing hard on my ass. I scooted us as close to the middle as I could so the sirens couldn't get us on either side of it.

I was breathing hard, but I was breathing. Alex, meanwhile, gasped every couple of seconds like he couldn't get enough air.

"Stay with me," I said. "Just... don't go to sleep."

"I might not have a choice," he murmured.

"Hold on. I'll... I'll figure something out."

I remembered some episode of *Grey's Anatomy* I'd watched about a million years ago. On one episode, someone was bleeding and the person with them had torn their clothes to make a tourniquet for them. I needed to do that for Alex or he wouldn't stand a chance.

I'd already torn and dirtied my clothes, so I had little to work with. I was thinking about infection, but I had to stop myself. He couldn't get infected if he bled out. I had to help him.

"Alex," I said, tugging at the bottom of my shirt until it gave way and peeled off in a long strip. "Alex, I swear to God. Please, don't leave me here. I don't want to be alone."

"I know," he said. "I just..."

His voice trailed off. I wasn't sure if it was fair to keep him talking, but I was afraid of what might happen if I didn't. If he fell unconscious, he might never wake up.

"Fuck," I muttered.

I could feel Harper's and Molly's eyes on us, but they couldn't get to us. We couldn't stay here forever, but for now, we were safe.

I took the strip of cloth I'd torn from my shirt and wrapped it around Alex's thigh. The sight of the wound made me gag, and I felt embarrassed about it. Then, I felt embarrassed for being embarrassed. We had enough shit to worry about.

I tied the shirt as tight as I could manage, my arms trembling with the effort. I wished I'd learned more about knots in my life. I wished I'd learned more about a lot in my life. Maybe it wasn't too late.

Alex had gotten too pale and too quiet. I touched his cheek and it was cold.

"Listen to me," I said, my voice pleading and frantic. "Alex, I need to tell you something."

His eyelids fluttered, but they didn't close. "If you're going to say you regret taking this job, I know." Alex's tone was playful, but it wasn't enough to detract from our dire circumstances.

"I should've told you earlier. I know that now," I said. I had to get the words out now or else I'd keep them. That was worse. "I love you, Alex. I mean, I'm... I'm *in love* with you. I think I always have been."

He tilted his face toward me, a smile stretching over his lips. "Somehow I always knew."

My heart clenched like a fist. He hadn't said it back. As pleased as he might've looked, he hadn't reciprocated.

" I needed you to know," I said.

A flush crept into my cheeks. Jesus. We were on the verge of death and I was still embarrassed by the concept of sharing my feelings. The human body was amazing.

"For what it's... for what it's worth," Alex said, "I'm in love with you, too."

My heart felt like it grew a thousand sizes in that moment. Relief broke over me, and I laughed, tears springing to my eyes. "We should've talked about this," I said.

"We're talking about it now," Alex said.

"You know what I mean."

Alex winced, clutching at his thigh. Blood soaked his pants and it was difficult to tell whether or not the wound was still bleeding. I wasn't sure the tourniquet was tight enough, but even if it was, he'd lost a lot of blood already. He was too weak to move, and I was too weak to carry him. Fear knifed my chest.

"I don't want to leave you here," I said, my voice breaking.

"I know you don't," he murmured. He was having a hard

time keeping his eyes open. "Liv, you did your best. You *loved* me. You don't know what that means to me."

"*Love*," I insisted. "Present tense."

"Not for too much longer."

"Don't say that," I said.

"Okay," Alex said. "I won't."

The air between us stilled and silenced. I had no clue where the sirens were now, nor did I care. They were in the water, waiting. They had part of Alex's leg. My stomach tied itself into a knot. I raised my eyes to the ceiling of the bunker again, scanning for a crack or any signs of light.

I found one.

It was in the far corner a few feet behind us—a silver of light winking down from the ceiling.

"Alex," I breathed.

"Come here," he said. In a minute I was in his arms and he was kissing me. His lips were cracked but so were mine and it didn't even matter. I'd wanted this for years.

Our timing was awful. If only we'd known.

When we broke apart I was crying again, tears streaming down my cheeks and splashing against my shirt, probably cutting paths in the dirt on my skin, but I couldn't see myself to confirm it.

Alex rested his forehead against mine. He was still smiling.

"We should've done that more often," he said.

"We'll do it when we get out of here," I said. "We can kiss and fool around and whatever else you want."

"That sounds nice," he said, but his voice was far away.

I touched his cheek again. It was clammy. His forehead slipped away from mine, his head lolling against his chest.

"Alex," I said.

"I'm here," he muttered.

"Don't leave me here alone. I might have found a way out."

"You can't travel with me and you know it," he countered.

"Liv, you're just... you're just too nice to say it. We both know what has to happen."

I sniffled, lifting my other hand to cradle his face. Gently, I guided his chin up so he was looking into my eyes. "I won't leave you," I said.

"Then I'll have to leave you," he said. "Cause a big enough distraction for you to escape."

"No."

He didn't say anything else, but he kept looking at me. We both knew that *cause a big enough distraction* meant *sacrifice myself*. He was still willing to die to help me make it out of there alive. No one had ever loved me like that before. I didn't think I'd ever find a love like that again. Another tide of tears spilled from my eyes. The salt burned my dry skin, but in a way, it was atonement.

My eyes felt like they were on fire. I couldn't stop crying. He pressed his mouth to mine again, and I sighed against his lips.

"Alex," I breathed against his mouth.

"You can't talk me out of this," he said. "If I... if I can get you out of here alive, I'll do whatever it takes."

I thought about walking into the bunker, about getting in the boats, abot discovering the sirens. I thought about watching them murder my friends, and watching Alex put Claire out of her misery. Grief knifed my chest. Guilt followed close behind.

Why did I deserve to make it out alive more than anyone else did?

I hadn't pursued what I loved. I hadn't tried to make a difference in the world.

"Tell my mom I'm sorry," Alex murmured.

"Are you?" I asked.

"No," he said. "But tell her, anyway. She'll need closure."

"What about me?"

"What *about* you, Liv?" He pulled back and searched my face. His eyebrows knitted together. "You're not changing my mind here. I told you."

I felt so far beyond crying at that point, but I didn't have the strength to do anything else. My chest hurt so bad I wasn't sure it would ever feel better again. And the worst part of it all was that Alex was still here. How would I react as soon as he was gone?

I couldn't dwell on that. I needed to enjoy the time we had together.

Something stirred the surface of the water, most likely a fin. I swallowed.

The sirens were getting restless.

"Listen," Alex hissed. "I'll... I'll get in the water. You take care of the rest, okay?"

I felt like someone had poured a whole anthill inside my body. My nerve endings were on fire.

"Olivia," he said. "I need an answer."

My gaze darted back to the light in the ceiling, the sliver I was about to stake both of our fates on. I nodded. Alex squeezed my hand.

"I'm not blaming you for this," he said. "I hope you never think that."

Why was he handling this so gracefully? Somehow, that only made it worse. He should've been angry, upset, crying, screaming —but he comforted me instead.

That was why I loved him.

"I'm sorry," I said.

"You have nothing to be sorry for."

But I did, and I was sorry for all of it then.

"Go," he murmured.

"Alex—"

"Liv," he said. "Please."

I put my arms around him and held him close, not caring that he was bleeding on me. I wanted to close my eyes, but I knew I couldn't because then I wouldn't be able to memorize his face.

This wasn't how I would've chosen to remember Alex, but it was all I'd get. There would be no second chances for us anymore.

I lifted his head to kiss him. Then I steeled myself and pulled away. He offered me a lopsided smile.

Before he said another word, I mentally planned my next steps. With the sirens distracted, I'd slip into the water, swim toward the seam on the other side, and climb my way up there before they could do anything about it.

Alex was the distraction. I tried not to dwell on that part.

"I love you," I said.

"Go, Liv. Get out."

Although it was one of the hardest things I've ever had to do, I let go of him then. He was right. This was the only way that I could ever make it out.

I swallowed again like I could somehow get the shit out of my throat, the feeling of dread that had perpetually worn me down the past few days or however the fuck long we'd been down there, as if I could ever forget the horrors I'd seen. It all flashed through my head again—Ben, Ryan, Claire. Alex. Grief squeezed my heart like someone trying to squeeze water from a stone.

I knew what I had to do. That didn't mean it was easy.

Before any other feeling got the better of me, I slipped off the platform into the water. The splash of Alex doing the same stung me like a wasp, but I had to keep going.

"Hey, bitches," Alex called. "You can't even finish the job right, can you? I'm still fucking alive."

My heart clawed at my voice box. I wanted to yell at Alex then, to call the whole thing off, but I knew it was pointless. I knew that I had to keep going. I refused to let Alex's sacrifice be in vain.

Once I heard a series of loud splashes, I pushed off the side of the platform and kicked my way toward the opposite wall, where a small ledge stuck out enough for me to stand on.

Alex swore. It echoed off the walls of the bunker. There was more splashing. Some screaming. I tried to tune it out, to keep plunging ahead, to save myself from these fucking monsters like no one else had had the chance to.

Before the sirens even realized they'd swam into a trick, I was clambering up the ledge and searching for a handhold. Water dripped from me, making my clothes stick to my body. The brief plunge had washed some of Alex's blood off of me, but I didn't think it would ever truly wash away for good.

I glanced up at the ceiling, at the seam that held so much incredible promise.

There was more splashing. I couldn't hear screaming anymore.

"Fuck," I whispered bitterly. Then, my hand found a groove in the wall. I stood on tiptoe and stretched my fingers toward the ceiling. I pushed along the seam. The trap door opened.

I was free.

I don't know how I had the strength to climb out of the bunker. I guess it was adrenaline, or something like it. Something primal. Whatever the case, I got the fuck out of the bunker. I had made it out alive.

I took one last glance through the trapdoor at the water below. I spat through the hole and I closed it.

"Good fucking riddance," I said.

The harsh light of the sun stung my eyes after so much time in semidarkness. I squinted so hard I gave myself a headache. Once I'd put a hand up to stop the sun's assault on my eyes, the rest of the world kicked in. The air was cold, and since I was wet, the wind raised goosebumps on my skin. Cicadas whined in the distance. I could hear rustling leaves, chittering squirrels, and singing birds, too.

I was crying again. I only knew it because it was suddenly difficult to see through all the water in my eyes. I didn't know how I still had enough tears left to cry. It felt like a miracle.

Gradually, my eyes adjusted to the sun.

I let my hand fall by my side and surveyed my surroundings.

I was still in the forest. That was a good thing. The bunker was so big, I'd worried we were somewhere else, somewhere I wouldn't know how to get out of. But no, I was still in Dawsonville Forest, or else somewhere that looked an awful lot like it. It felt like a season had passed in the bunker, but the trees looked the same. Nothing had changed except me.

I touched my hair. Water and sticky blood plastered it to the side of my face.

Ben. Ryan. Claire. Alex.

Their names were a loop in the back of my mind, an itch I couldn't scratch.

I can still feel it in here.

My chest hurt so bad I feared I'd have a heart attack. Wouldn't that have been the cruelest form of poetry? To survive that whole hellish ordeal just to pass away from a human condition?

A clearing stood out nearby. I made my way toward it, not knowing where I was going or having any kind of plan. Once I got to the clearing, I reached for my cell phone out of habit—and, of course, it wasn't there. It must have fallen out in the bunker.

I've never been a huge fan of the outdoors. That probably makes me sound strange, but in light of everything else I've talked about, maybe it's the most normal thing about my situation. But there, standing in the middle of that clearing with the trees and air and sun, it felt transcendent—like I'd gotten the chance to step outside my body for a second and just look at everything.

It also felt like the first time I'd been able to take a breath in a very long time.

I allowed myself a moment there, and then I plotted my next move. I had no idea which part of the forest I was in. I had no compass, map, or GPS to guide me back to my car, assuming that my car was still there. Hitchhiking made the most sense.

I'd never hitchhiked in my life. You know, we grew up learning stranger danger and all of that, and I've consumed enough true crime content to know what a bad idea it is to get into a vehicle with someone you don't know. Still, having survived three killer mermaids, I figured I could take my chances with a single human being.

My gaze fell on a dirt path winding through the trees. I craned my neck to see the path's end, but I couldn't find it. I just had to go with it.

Before all this happened, I don't think I ever really trusted my instincts. Now, I'd stake my life on them, because I have already.

I brushed myself off like that would do anything about the blood. I took a deep breath. I started walking.

I had a hard time figuring out what to do once a car picked me up. I wasn't about to spill my guts about the sirens to just anyone. Trust me when I say I'm lucid enough to understand what a bad idea that would be.

Hell, I could barely get the words out to you.

ANDIE

"I know how bad this makes me look," Liv said. "How bad it makes me sound. I know that given the spectacular lack of physical evidence and the gross abundance of speculation, it doesn't look good for me."

I had to keep her talking. We were so close to the end.

"What happened next?" I asked.

"At the end of the path was a road," she continued. "Driving up the road was a cream-colored Toyota Corolla with a woman inside who looked about my parents' age. Her frizzy red hair stuck out in all directions. I convinced her to pick me up. When she stopped the car, she rolled the window down. She looked me over. She was nervous. Fidgety."

"Were you aware of your appearance?" I asked.

"I didn't have a mirror, but I knew I looked rough," Liv said. "Blood bloomed over my shirt and pants. I'm sure I looked like shit. I didn't blame her for being anxious. She asked if I needed an ambulance. I told her probably, but then I had her bring me here."

We sat there in silence. It was so quiet I could hear the fluorescent lights buzzing overhead. It was, as she'd said, one hell of a story. It was hard to believe her, yet somehow, I did.

I understood now why I'd been given this case. Liv reminded

me of Joy when we'd first met—vulnerable, hurt, and eager for someone to believe her.

Now, she had me. I would see this thing through with her.

Whatever that meant.

Liv opened her mouth to say something else, and the door swung open. Lyle and Anderson entered. Their faces were stony. Lyle bowed her head.

I got up from my chair. "What's going on?"

Neither of them needed to be there. I had everything under control.

I didn't know Anderson well, but he cut an imposing figure. At six foot four, he was the tallest man in the precinct. He was built like a tank. If Lyle had brought him with her, she must've thought she needed the muscle.

Why?

Goosebumps broke over my skin. Something wasn't right.

"Miss Reyes," Lyle said, "have you been read your rights before entering this interrogation?"

"Interrogation?" Liv's eyes flashed. "We were just talking."

My heart jumped into my throat. "Hey, what's this about?"

"Olivia Reyes, you have the right to remain silent."

Shock froze my intestines. "What are you doing?"

This had to be a mistake. No way this was happening.

I couldn't move. Lyle read Liv her rights while Anderson pulled her hands behind her back and cuffed her.

"Anything you say can be used against you in a court of law," Lyle continued. "You have the right to talk to a lawyer for advice before we ask you any questions. You have the right to have a lawyer present during questioning. If you cannot afford a lawyer, one will be appointed for you. If you decide to answer questions now without a lawyer present, you have the right to stop answering and request counsel at any time."

"Clarissa, please," I said. This couldn't be happening, not after everything we'd been through, not after everything Liv had suffered.

Liv wasn't looking at me. She refused to meet my gaze.

"Andie, I tried to warn you," Lyle said. "Chief tried to warn you, too. It's too late. We're remanding her into custody pending her trial. She'll be in the county jail."

Rage and fear bubbled up inside me. "Who signed off on this?"

Lyle sighed. "Chief Alameda, like I told you."

Something wasn't adding up.

"Why would he do that?" I asked. "This is my case. He put me on it himself."

"Things have changed," Lyle said.

"What are you talking about?" I asked.

"We tested the clothes she came in with. Ran them through the analyzer at the lab."

"Don't say anything else until we can get you a lawyer," I warned Liv. Then, to Lyle: "What is it? What aren't you telling me here?"

"What did you find?" Liv asked.

"Liv, please," I said.

"Blood," Lyle said. "A lot of it. And none of it was hers."

"Fuck you," Liv retorted. "There's no *way* none of it was mine. You know what I've been through."

"Most of it belongs to Alexander Dang. There are also traces of DNA from Claire Thibodeaux and Benjamin and Ryan Jenkins."

Lyle looked at me like this should've meant something, and maybe it should have. But it made sense considering everything Liv had told me.

"So they bled on her," I said.

"It's more than that, Andie."

Wesson came into the room to assist Lyle. He looked incredibly uncomfortable standing in the doorway with his hands in his pockets. He didn't want to look at me either. When I'd asked him about Liv's whereabouts—about the security detail—had he known this was going to happen? Had they already been handling it?

I felt like he'd lied to my face. Weren't we better friends than that?

"Wesson," I hissed.

"My hands are tied here, McCollum."

McCollum, not Andie. He was distancing himself from me.

My stomach hurt. My chest hurt. I wanted to open my mouth and scream until this whole mess went away. But Liv was hurting, too, and I knew that. I had to do something about it.

"Do you have a lawyer?" I asked Liv.

"Get her out of here," Lyle told Wesson. "Andie, you're interfering. We could get you for obstruction."

"So do it," I said. Lyle sighed. Wesson took Liv by the shoulders and steered her out of the room. I had to follow them. I knew I couldn't, but I had to.

Nobody stopped me.

"We'll find you a lawyer," I told Liv in a breathless rush of an exhale. "We'll find you a lawyer and we'll fight this. I'll help you."

"Andie," Liv said. My name was a prayer on her lips.

"Andie," Lyle said. My name was a curse on hers.

I knew I needed to back down. That's what everyone expected me to do. That's what the old Andie might've done, the one who married her high school sweetheart to shake off her small town's disdain. The one who'd become a police officer because it was expected of her, not because she was passionate about law enforcement or about keeping the streets "clean."

"I'll go to the chief," I continued.

"Go," said Wesson. "Please."

Automatically, I reached for Liv's hand. Then, I remembered she was in handcuffs, and I felt like an idiot. I felt like they'd taken something important from me.

I could only think of one course of action, beyond looking for a lawyer, which would only buy us time. I knew Dad well enough to understand that if we were remanding Liv into custody, it meant there was always a solid case against her. They'd done me a favor telling me about the blood. I didn't know what else they'd found.

I needed to find out.

Whatever it took, I was going to mount an investigation into Liv's claims. I'd go to the bunker myself if I had to. Of course, anything I found on my own and not at the discretion of the precinct's jurisdiction wouldn't be admissible as evidence in court.

Cold fear washed over me then. Something I hadn't considered already—because there'd originally been no criminal charges filed against Liv—was that her statement might not even be admissible. I was personally involved. That fucked the whole thing up. I wasn't objective, and I did the bulk of the interviewing on my own. They could throw the whole thing out. Hell, depending on the judge's mood, they could even dismiss the material Liv had given us when Lyle was in the room, too.

Shit.

I didn't have a choice. I needed to look for the bunker.

With another glance at Liv, I turned on my heel and headed upstairs to Dad's office. The door was wide open and he didn't look up when I hurried in.

He'd been expecting me. Of course he had. He knew me.

"You can't change my mind," he said without looking up from the file on his desk. "If she were anyone else, Andie, you'd be asking me to do this."

"She's not anyone else," I said.

"No, or you wouldn't be here." At last, he looked up at me. His eyebrows knitted together the way they always did when he was concerned about me or when he thought I was making a reckless decision. "Andie... Andrea, I'm tired. This whole case has exhausted me. I know you're tired, too."

The way he was speaking implied that he'd paid closer attention to the Reyes incident than I'd realized. I stood behind the chair in front of his desk, settling my fingers on the back of it.

"I left Joy," I told him.

"For her?" he asked.

"For me," I said. "She's just a bonus."

He wasn't changing my mind, and this wasn't a phase. I needed to make him understand both those things.

"Who's looking to verify her statement?" I asked.

"I've spent enough resources on this already," Dad said. "If Ms. Reyes finds a lawyer to defend her, we'll work with the prosecution to determine a plan of action."

It was a half answer, and wholly unsatisfying.

"I want to stay on the case," I said.

"I can't let you do that."

"So don't let me, then," I said. "I'll go, anyway."

Dad shuffled the papers and set the file aside to focus his attention on me. He sighed, and I knew there was a tide of bureaucratic bullshit coming. He was taking off the Dad hat and putting on the cop one. I knew that I wouldn't like whatever he had to say, and I steeled myself to receive it.

"I would lead an investigation myself if I thought it would make any difference," he started. "I can't show favoritism. You've always known that."

I did. But I wasn't asking for favoritism now.

"Let me do it," I said.

"I already told you I can't spend more department resources on this." He steepled his fingers. "Besides that, I think you need a few days off."

I frowned at him. "Why would I need time off?"

"You might not have a choice," he said. Dread churned in my stomach. I'd never been suspended or placed on leave before. I honestly hadn't thought it would happen to me. It seemed to be imminent now.

"I won't just roll over and take it," I said.

"Hand over your gun and your badge, please. I don't want to ask you again."

Rage simmered under the surface of my skin. "You can't stop

me from going there. You know that."

"I do," he said. "But... I can't help you out. You can help yourself by following protocol. Please."

Angrily, I unclipped my holster and set it and the gun down on his desk. I took off my badge and slid it over to him as well. Without them, I felt naked. Heat rushed to my cheeks—from anger or embarrassment, I couldn't say.

"Go home," Dad said.

"What if I don't know where that is anymore?" My voice was high. Tight. Broken. I barely recognized it.

"Whatever you and Joy have been through, I'm sure she'd still be there for you," he said. *Like I can't be for you now*, he didn't say. "Unless you think the situation isn't safe?"

I almost snorted. There'd never been even an inkling of violence in our relationship. Joy wasn't even into anything rough in the bedroom.

"It's fine," I said. Then, because I couldn't help myself, "I don't need your help. You've been helpful already."

He didn't stop me from walking out of the office. He didn't even try. He knew me better than that.

ANDIE

I slammed the front door behind me. Joy sat at the bar in the kitchen, eating tomato soup and a grilled cheese sandwich. She frowned at me. "I thought you had work," she said.

"I did," I said. "He suspended me."

Her eyes widened and she set down the spoon. "What? What did you do?"

"I didn't do anything," I said. "It was what I wanted to do that was the problem." I got a glass out of the cabinet and went over to the fridge to fill it with water from the door. The ice cubes tumbled in and clinked against the rim. One fell to the floor. I stooped to pick it up, sighing. "I don't want to talk about it."

"What happened to her?" Joy asked softly.

"I said I didn't want to talk about it." I tossed the ice cube into the sink. "I'm just... I'm so pissed."

Joy stared into the depths of her soup. "Is it because of that Reyes woman?"

"Yeah." She couldn't just leave it alone. Then, it dawned on me—maybe I could use her help.

Dad had barred me from using any more department resources. I knew better than to try to reach out to any of my coworkers for aid. But Joy wasn't on the force. Joy would have my back.

131

"She's... she's in trouble," I told Joy, sitting down beside her at the bar. "They found some evidence. Without going too in-depth, she's in custody now. Not just protective."

"So, she's going to trial," Joy finished.

"Yeah, I guess so. As far as I know, she doesn't have a lawyer, either." I reached up and massaged the back of my neck, groaning. "All we have to go on—beyond the physical evidence—are Liv's statements. And, unfortunately, mostly, I'm the only one she talked to."

"Hmm." Joy drummed her fingers on the bar. "What about Lyle?"

"She wants no part in this." I didn't know that for sure, but it was a safe assumption. She'd treated me like persona non grata and had barely even looked at me while they apprehended Liv.

"And you can't ask anyone else because of the suspension," Joy said.

"No," I confirmed.

"Shit," Joy said. I looked at her plate. She'd left the crusts of her sandwich to the side, just like always. I picked up a piece and popped it into my mouth. As I chewed, I considered my options again. "What are you thinking, then?" Joy asked. "Do you want to investigate it further?" she pressed. "Can you even do that?"

"I don't know," I said, swallowing. "All I know is that I want to. I think... well, Joy, I think I need your help."

"I'll say," she said.

I reached for the other crust, and she didn't stop me. Joy knew I needed help. She knew she was the only person in the world who could see my side of the story—besides Liv herself, and Liv couldn't help me verify her claims.

My cup of water sat undisturbed. I picked it up and sipped from it, at a loss for anything else to say or do that would make this situation feel even remotely normal.

"If you need my help," Joy started.

I let my shoulders drop. "You already know I do."

"I'm not sure what I can do, but... I'm still your friend,

Andie. I'll do whatever you need me to do, okay? That's a promise."

"This wasn't exactly in our wedding vows," I said. "I understand if you want to bow out."

"Those don't quite count anymore. Anyway, I'm in." She offered me a smile, and it felt more genuine than others she'd given me lately. "So, what's our plan of attack?"

That was a good question. I didn't know.

According to Liv's story, it was not just difficult to get into the bunker—it was illegal, full stop. I wasn't even sure we could set foot in the forest without getting into trouble. For all I knew, Dad would be waiting there for me to show up.

"Shit," I muttered.

Joy picked up her spoon and stuck it in the soup but let go of it instead of bringing it to her mouth. She rested her hands in her lap. "What are we trying to prove here, Andie?"

I took a deep breath. "They're accusing her of murder, Joy. All I have to use against them are her statements, and that's not enough."

"We need to find physical evidence," Joy said. "Right?"

She always knew which station my train of thought would stop at. "Yes, and if we don't... I don't know what will happen."

It felt strange being so open with Joy now after we'd spent years keeping our secrets and our feelings from each other. I couldn't help wondering if this kind of honesty a lot sooner might have saved our marriage. I didn't have the time to dwell on it now, though.

"It's dangerous," I said. "We need to go into Dawsonville Forest. We have to find a bunker, and then we'll go inside." I hesitated. "A lot of it is flooded. And... radioactive."

I left out the sirens. She could see them for herself. I'd already given her too much to consider.

I made a mental list of everything we'd need to bring so we could make sure we were ready—flashlights, snorkel or scuba gear if possible, boots, maybe some kind of weapon. I hated that I didn't have my gun anymore. As seldom as I'd shot it, I felt comfortable around it. Safe and secured. Protected. Now, I felt wide open in the worst way possible. I had no clue what was in store for us once we got down there.

I hoped to God Liv was telling the truth. If she wasn't—

But she was.

"Once we do this," I said, "there's no going back. If we get into trouble—"

"I know," Joy said. "My mind's made up."

I held my tongue. "Let's go then."

It took almost no time to get to the bunker. Neither of us talked much on the drive over. I wasn't sure there was anything that needed to be said.

We parked the car across the street from the chain-link fence and walked to the bunker together. Our fingers brushed, but we didn't hold hands.

I felt disconnected from my body in the forest, like I was just floating around overhead. My heart was still with Liv, whatever she was going through.

So, we found the bunker. We found a way in, too. I didn't know what we'd do once we were inside, but at least this was a start. A step in the right direction.

We weren't supposed to be here. The air all but screamed it.

ANDIE

I want to tell you what we found in the bunker. I want to tell you what we didn't.

We found human remains, bones picked clean and snapped in half, missing marrow, with scratches like teeth marks all over the place.

We also located the journal, which I planned to file with the rest of my reports.

But we never found any sirens.

From: **Andrea McCollum** <amccollum@dpd.gov>
To: **Roger Alameda** <ralameda@dpd.gov>
Subject: **RE: The Reyes Incident**

Mon, November 21, 2022, 2:35 PM

Chief Alameda,

Effective immediately, I am resigning from my
position at the Dawsonville Police Department. Thank you for the opportunity and the
lessons I have learned along the way.

If there is any way I can be of help during
this transition, please reach out.

Regards,
Sergeant Andrea McCollum

About the Author

Briana Morgan is a horror author and playwright. Her books include *Mouth Full of Ashes*, *The Tricker-Treater and Other Stories*, *Unboxed: A Play*, and more. Her short stories can be found in various anthologies. She's also a proud member of the Horror Writers Association.

Briana lives with her partner and two cats in Atlanta, Georgia.

Also by Briana Morgan

A Tricker-Treater Christmas

Mouth Full of Ashes

The Tricker-Treater and Other Stories

Unboxed

The Writer's Guide to Slaying Social

Livingston Girls

Reflections

Touch

Blood and Water

Printed in Great Britain
by Amazon